WIN
AMERIC

NATIONAL PLAYWRITING AWARD

(SECOND PLACE)

AND

NATIONAL SELECTION TEAM FELLOWSHIP
AWARD

"One of the most intelligently written plays I have
read in a decade."
— Gary Garrison, KCACTF Playwriting Chair/
Dramatists Guild President

"One of the best original plays I've seen."
— Gregg Henry, KCACTF Artistic Director

"Mahonri Stewart, remember that name. . . a tremendous debut."
— Eric Samuelsen, *Irreantum Magazine*

"*Farewell to Eden* is a uniquely rewarding character study that is so splendidly played as to make it highly recommended."
— Blair Howell, *Deseret News*

"Witty banter, symbolism, broad range of characters, historical figures popping in and out, romantic stories that avoid clichés, and did I mention witty banter and fully fleshed out characters? Please sign me up."
— Kara Henry, *Front Row Reviewers*

"A thought provoking experience for anyone who catches *Farewell to Eden*."
— Russell Warne, *Utah Theatre Bloggers Association*

"*Farewell to Eden* is brilliant. It's complicated, not very predictable, and has a lot of depth and characterization."
— Sharon Haddock, *Deseret News*

Published by: Prospero Arts and Media

Text Design by: Mahonri Stewart

Cover Photo by: Greg Deakins

ISBN: 9781696322669

For performance rights to *Farewell to Eden***, contact Leicester
Bay Theatrical Licensing at https://leicesterbaytheatricals.
com/ or Prospero Arts and Media at prosperoarts@gmail.
com.**

Mahonri Stewart is an award winning playwright, screenwriter, poet, novelist, director, producer, and educator. He has written over two dozen plays, most of which have been produced throughout the U.S. and Europe, including productions in Los Angeles, Scotland, and Switzerland. His premiere play *Farewell to Eden* won the Kennedy Center's American College Theater Festival's National Playwriting Award (Second Place) and their National Selection Team Fellowship Award. He has also received numerous other awards and honors for his plays and screenplays, including a ScreenCraft Finalist award for his screenplay *Wrightsborough*. He received his Master of Fine Arts degree in Dramatic Writing from Arizona State University and his Bachelor's degree in Theatre Arts from Utah Valley University. He's a former Playwright in Residence at the Noorda Regional Theater for Childern and Youth.

FAREWELL TO EDEN

A PLAY BY MAHONRI STEWART

REVISED EDITION

FAREWELL TO EDEN

by Mahonri Stewart

Farewell to Eden premiered at Utah Valley State College (now Utah Valley University) on November 13-22, 2003. It also played at California State University: San Bernardino in February, 2003, for the Kennedy Center American College Theatre Festival.

Georgiana Highett	Margie Johnson
Stephen Lockhart	Aaron Wilden
Thomas Highett	Brandon Michael West
Catherine Highett	Amber James
Darrel Fredericks	Samuel Snow Schofield
Mary	Angela Youmans
Harold Lowe	Kenneth F. Brown
Esther Whitefield	Tatum Langton
Hannah Whitefield	Fallon R. Hanson
Brigham Young	Sam Davis
John Taylor	Russ Bennett
Director	James Arrington
Production Manager	Tiffany Shaw
Stage Manager	Sarah Dawn Lowry
Assistant Stage Managers	Chelsea Cordell, Daniel Whiting
Costume Designer	Mary Haddock
Wardrobe	Cassie Hinkson
Set Designer	Randy Seely
Lighting Designer	Brett Larson

Sound Designer	Don Christensen
Technical Director	Erika Smock
Assistant Technical Director	Marisa Hernandez
Props Master	Daniel Whiting
Makeup Designer	Beth Hill
Hair and Wigs	Hillary Scroeder
Scene Shop Foreman	Steve Purdy
Costume Shop Manager	Camille Jackson Morris
House Manager	Aurora Borjas
Light Board Operator	Rebecca Peterson
Sound Board Operator	Brian Randall
Master Electrician	Devan Byrne

Stage Crew Bryce Bishop, Daniel Whiting, Devan Byrne, Erika Smock, Burke Simmons, Bryan Taylor, Joni Martin, Mile McVey, Shayne Hudson, Don Christensen

Set Construction Daniel Whiting, Randy Seely, Erika Smock, Burke Simmons, Bryan Taylor, Joni Martin, Mike McVey, Shayne Hudson, Don Christensen

Costume Builders Angela Youmans, Caleb Van Bloem, Erin Neilson, Sarah Hunt, Shayne Hudson, Melissa Kmetch, Collette Maxwell, Mikelle Smiley, Marlene Neptune, Lori Baird

Make-up Arists Angela Peterson, Rachel Bean, Brianne Buckley, Courtney Beam, Ryan Templeman, Brittany Treadwell

Female Dressers Diana Jex, Melissa Christensen, Colette Maxwell

Male Dressers Tyler Park, Russ Bennett

FOREWORD

"Ladies and Gentlemen, we have a playwright!" I shouted and slammed my hand down on a nearby desk. The startled students of my Introduction to Theatre class at Utah Valley University had never seen me do this. Heck, I had never seen me do this.

As a university professor, I regularly taught the class, hoping to elevate interest in and appreciation for theatre as an artform. As one of the base requirements of the class, all students were required to write a ten-minute (one scene, ten pages) play. In preparation we studied simple dramatic structure, how a play should look on the page (formatting), and then, with a little coaxing and a leap of faith (and a deadline and a grade), most students could produce a little comic or dramatic scene with a beginning, middle, and an end.

Most of these little plays were mundane, some were obviously movies (couldn't be done on a stage), and a few failed so hilariously I could hardly finish reading them, but I read them anyway; part of my grading. All the while, I was secretly looking for that "diamond in the rough" that all professors dream of; that one student that exceeds all expectations and that, with training and persistence, can create something quite stout and beautiful.

They didn't come along often, you know, that raw, unfound talent. Perhaps someone who didn't know they had any sense for drama, or suddenly found they had an unusual eye for character, or perhaps an ear for wry dialogue. Occasionally a student woke up and was genuinely surprised to find out that writing wasn't drudgery, but fun, engaging, and even lightning in their soul. That creative moment unlocked something in their souls they'd never known before. It was a striking and wonderful moment.

But this was different. When we read Mahonri Stewart's ten-minute play *The Fortress** aloud in class, it became more and more obvious to me that this was a rare and special piece. This was not a hesitant talent, this was not an accidental ability, this was a true

---

*   Stewart and Arrington are unsure what the original working title was, the play went through so many. *The Subtle Beauty, The Word of the Subtle Soul, The Fortress, The Children of the Father* were all considered before deciding on *Farewell to Eden*.

discovery of a gift—like accidentally shoveling into a vein of gold. The scene itself was thoughtful, dramatic, carefully drawn, full of suspense. And how did this bright, shiny, squeaky-clean, grinning kid produce this terrific, powerful, and resolute female lead character?! Impressive.

So, I made my pronouncement in a loud Shakespearean voice, slammed the desk and alarmed the nearly somnambulant students. I could hardly wait till the end of class to speak to this young man for I knew this moment had put us on a collision course with something wonderful.

As I remember it, the conversation went something like this:

Me: This is part of a larger work, isn't it?
Mahonri: *(A grinning, slight hesitation)* … Well, yeah.
Me: Is it already written?
Mahonri: Ha, ha—well, not yet.
Me: But this is a slice of it, right?
Mahonri: Yeah, yeah. It is.
Me: Okay, great. Well, how would you feel about writing the rest of it?
Mahonri: Really?!
Me: If it's good enough we could produce it in the department.
Mahonri: *(Distant look)* Wow. Yeah, okay. Uh, okay! I'll see what I can do.
At that point I wasn't certain the play would actually

be finished. If so, I wasn't certain how long or torturous the experience of getting it producible might be. I wasn't even sure I could convince my colleagues to put the time and effort into a final event. Wasn't certain I believed it myself, but that strange and faith-filled path is exactly what ALL productions must go through. It's almost religious in nature, starting with a seed of hope and some ideas printed on paper, then everyone along the way must manifest faith in the possible outcome. However, at that early point, all I actually knew was that I had found what I thought, what I hoped was a new talent. I'm pleased to say I wasn't wrong.

Suddenly, early that summer after the late-in-the-semester of discovery, Mahonri actually produced a full-length, readable version. I was astounded! (I have since learned that Mahonri is the fastest writer, editor, and rewriter I've ever run in to.) The finished play, later renamed *Farewell to Eden*, hung together, the plot was thick, the characters were interesting. Though it wasn't perfect, the script had all the major components to make it juicy and workable. Over the course of the next year we went through many writes, rewrites, and changes. We eventually pulled in at something like ten rewrites.

To give the reader an understanding of Mahonri's dedication and speed, I remember reading the play and seeing that from the end of one scene to the beginning of the next (lights out, lights up), the leading lady had to change from one costume to another. Realizing, because of the style of the 19th century outfits that there wouldn't possibly be the amount of time necessary to make such a change I pointed it out to Mahonri. He understood and we talked over some possible ways to either extend the scene without the leading lady or start the following scene before she arrived. The very next day, if memory serves me correctly, Mahonri had written a short scene following the exit of the leading lady that is still one of my favorite little scenes in the entire play! Two characters that I wouldn't have dreamed could have a useful interaction made a short character statement with humor that added to the play and didn't just serve as a time waster. Boom!

I managed to convince my department of the opportunity at hand, adding that we could enter it into the Kennedy Center American College Theatre Festival (KCACTF), which is a nationwide organization of which we were in the Western section (Region 8). Our department had been invited to send one play to the festival years before and this would be our second effort.

It's often said, "When the student is ready, the teacher appears." In this case, it was the magnificent cast that materialized. People we hadn't seen and didn't know came out of the woodwork to create a perfect blend of characters for *Farewell to Eden*. Student designers had been carefully chosen to do the artwork of costumes, lighting, sound, and set. And finally, the show was ready for presentation. It was a wonderful collaboration and became a great hit. Fingers crossed.

The visiting adjudicators from KCACTF couldn't have been more impressed, leveling praise at Mahonri, the cast, the set, and the production values. One of the adjudicators from the University of the Pacific compared the lead character to Blanche Dubois from Tennessee Williams' *A Streetcar Named Desire*, commending Mahonri's character work. He said that he hoped for a bright future for Mahonri in the theatre, but that "we'll probably lose him to film and television."

We were thus invited to bring the show to the Regional Festival at California State University: San Bernardino. The students' set and costume designs were also recognized, and Margie Johnson's portrayal of Georgiana Highett was commended, as she and other students of ours were invited to compete in their Irene Ryan acting competition. During a meeting which Mahonri and I had with NYU's Gary Garrison, the playwriting chair for KCACTF and the Dramatists Guild President, Garrison told Mahonri that *Farewell to Eden* was the "most intelligently written script" he had read in a decade.

It was a big deal for our whole department and that wasn't the end. Mahonri was then selected as runner-up for the National Student Playwriting Award and received the National Selection Team Fellowship Award for Region 8, for which he was flown to Washington D.C. to participate in the National Festival at the Kennedy Center and receive his awards.

That was only the beginning. Mahonri Stewart wrote another successful play while at UVU, *Legends of Sleepy Hollow*, which won the Ruth and Nathan Hale Comedy Playwriting Award (Mahonri took both prizes that year, *Farewell to Eden* winning second place in the Hale Centre Theatre sponsored contest). After graduating, Mahonri eventually entered the Dramatic Writing (playwriting/screenwriting) Masters of Fine Arts degree at Arizona State University.

To my knowledge, Mahonri has had his plays produced by UVU, ASU, international theatre festivals in Los Angeles, Scotland, and Sweden, numerous high schools, and he often produces his own works through his theatre company, since theatrical producers are few and far between in his native Utah. He has authored more than two dozen plays; he has written numerous film and TV scripts; and is working on a myriad of other projects in various genres that are hard to keep up with!

I am happy to count Mahonri as one of my friends and colleagues, and I am honored to have slammed my hand down on the desk in that classroom many years ago.

- JAMES ARRINGTON, 2019

James Arrington (front center), Mahonri Stewart (far left), the original cast, and the set movers (dressed as servants). Courtesy of the UVU Department of Theatrical Arts.

Dedicated to James Arrington,
a trusted mentor and friend.
He did so much to encourage and improve this play —
and this playwright.

"The last few hours were certainly very painful," replied Anne: "but when pain is over, the remembrance of it often becomes a pleasure. One does not love a place the less for having suffered in it."

Jane Austen, *Persuasion*

Margie Johnson as Georgiana Highett. Photo courtesy of the UVU Department of Theatrical Arts.

Act One

SCENE ONE

TIME: 1840
PLACE: Edenbridge, England

The Highett Household, a wealthy home, well furnished and a portrait hanging above the mantelplace. The portrait is of Alexander Highett, now deceased. Enter GEORGIANA HIGHETT, CATHERINE HIGHETT, THOMAS HIGHETT, *and* HAROLD LOWE. GEORGIANA *is "high born," but perceives herself as plain. Her dress is severe and shows no sign of lace or embroidery.* THOMAS *is well dressed, but more colorfully, sometimes even flamboyant.* CATHERINE *has a distinct beauty to her.* HAROLD *is a dignified gentleman of the upper classes. All three of them wear black arm bands for mourning.*

HAROLD. A very sad business, Georgiana.
GEORGIANA. We do appreciate your kindness in
       visiting us so often, Harold. I know that
       Father found great comfort in you after
       Mother's death.
HAROLD. Susan — he wept like a child over her.
       The only tears I ever saw him shed.
GEORGIANA.   What you have done for our family
       will not be forgotten.
HAROLD.   And I find great comfort in all of you.
       Your father's death will not be the end of the

1

Highett line.

THOMAS. Yes, the torch must go on and all that.

HAROLD. I assume you are managing the estate, Thomas? You have a good sense for it?

THOMAS. I make an effort.

HAROLD. Along with your Father's business ventures?

THOMAS. It is complex work.

CATHERINE. Well, I do not see why you bother to carry on with Father's silly hobbies.

THOMAS. Father cared very much about his business projects. I—I want to honor that.

HAROLD. Thomas—you are not your normally spirited self.

CATHERINE. Please, do not encourage him back into his silliness! He is the worst person to take to parties. It is like having a *jester* at a ball! He is good for entertainment, but you never ask him to dance the minuet. Never.

THOMAS. *(An impish smile growing:)* We were able to get the wine out of Miss Kyle's dress. I do not see what the big to-do was! For a woman with such a tiny mouth, Miss Kyle certainly could scream loudly.

HAROLD. Well, you are a very different man than your Father, that is certain.

THOMAS. You are right there, Mr. Lowe—excuse me. I have much to do today. Miss Fields and I have made a kite. A very big one.
(Exit THOMAS.)

CATHERINE. I wish you wouldn't encourage Thomas

in Father's old habits, Mr. Lowe. People talked, you know they did. A baronet like Father doing all that — work. It was practically unpatriotic!

HAROLD. Your Father had great admiration for 'Captains of Industry' like me, Miss Catherine.

CATHERINE. Oh, don't misunderstand me, Mr. Lowe, I admire you, too — but that doesn't mean I am going to work at your presses.

HAROLD. Oh, but did you see the passion he put into his shipping business! It made him happy.

CATHERINE. People said it was beneath his class.

GEORGIANA. Catherine, when you become as noble as Father was, you simply do what you want. It is the aristocratic privilege.

CATHERINE. I swear, no one in this family knows what it requires to be a public figure!

HAROLD. Well, how are you faring then, Catherine?

CATHERINE. We are slowly easing ourselves back into society.

GEORGIANA. A little too slowly for her. Not even Catherine has been able to stomach such things at a time like this. It was the first instance I had ever seen her miss a dance. That was more earth shattering than if Parliament had suddenly been invaded by the French.

CATHERINE. And, of course, you are back to your sharp tongue.

HAROLD. Well, at least you all have survived with your humors intact.

CATHERINE. Ah, the wit of intelligent company heals all wounds. Isn't that right, Georgiana?

GEORGIANA. I wouldn't know, you havenot said an intelligent thing for years.

HAROLD. It looks like things are back to status quo then. All is well.

GEORGIANA. No, Harold, we've still much to pass through until our mourning is done.

HAROLD. You are truly your father's daughter.

CATHERINE. And what does that make me?

GEORGIANA. You father's *other* daughter.

CATHERINE. Excuse me, Mr. Lowe, but there is a new family in the neighborhood. I must not wait too long to leave my card.

(CATHERINE *shoots* GEORGIANA *a pointed look.*)

It would be rude.

(*Exit* CATHERINE.)

HAROLD. He was so proud of what you were becoming, Georgiana. He used to tell me all sorts of stories. Always bragging and bullying about his daughter. I hear that you've made quite the name for yourself. The president of Edenbridge's debating society. On the council for the Philosophical Association. A political advocate. You occupy prominent positions. Especially for a woman.

GEORGIANA. Yes, *for a woman*. You might as well put me in a zoo of rare species. Along with the unicorns and the phoenixes. Right now I am a spectacle, a curiosity. Nothing more.

HAROLD. I have something here for you, Georgiana.

(HAROLD *takes out a rectangular box and hands it to* GEORGIANA.)

GEORGIANA. For me?

CATHERINE. What is it?

HAROLD. Open it.

> (GEORGIANA *opens the box to find an ornately carved*
> *dagger.)*

GEORGIANA. Whatever could you have — oh! It —
it is magnificent.

HAROLD. Your father gave it to me.

GEORGIANA. Truly?

HAROLD. He said, "Keep it sharp, Harold. Keep it
sharp. Cut off all those that oppose you with a
keen, dangerous wit. Dissect their logic, dig out
their arguments, slice through all of their
defenses." I think it is appropriate to pass it
onto you now, Georgiana.

GEORGIANA. Thank you. I will stay true to the gift.

HAROLD. You will do great things. There will be
those who try to stop you. Just remember that
you are a stronger force and a keener mind.

GEORGIANA. A Highett.

HAROLD. A Highett. But I ought to leave now, if I
am to make it back to London in time.

GEORGIANA. Thomas! Catherine! Mr. Lowe is
leaving! I cannot thank you enough, Mr. Lowe.
You have been very thoughtful.

> (*Enter* THOMAS *and* CATHERINE.*)*

HAROLD. You are very welcome, my dear.

THOMAS. Goodbye, Mr. Lowe.

CATHERINE. Goodbye.

HAROLD. Farewell to you all, for now.

> (*Exit* HAROLD.*)*

CATHERINE. What is that?

GEORGIANA. A dagger that belonged to father.

CATHERINE. So why do you get it?

GEORGIANA. Obviously, Mr. Lowe thinks the symbolism applies to me. You are not sharp enough to cut bread.

CATHERINE. It is a family heirloom. He came to see me, too, after all.

GEORGIANA. Did he? To publish your autobiography perhaps? My my, that would be fascinating reading. Chapter One, "Our noble heroine gets up and does her hair." Chapter Two, "Our estimable heroine goes to a dinner party." Chapter Three, "Our majestic heroine goes into town to buy a hat!"

THOMAS. Oh, stop it, you two. May I see it, Georgiana?

(THOMAS *inspects the dagger curiously.*)

THOMAS. My, it is a rather frightening looking thing.

GEORGIANA. It is noble.

(THOMAS *lunges forward with the dagger.*)

THOMAS. Tally ho!

GEORGIANA. Oh, do be careful with it, you silly boy!

CATHERINE. Boys and their toys. You are such a sparrow, Thomas.

(THOMAS *brandishes the dagger about, swiping it in the air and playing at a mock battle.*)

THOMAS. Nice, this is nice.

(*Considering the dagger.*)

Just think of it — Thomas the Conqueror! Does the dagger match my shoes?

GEORGIANA. I think it is time to give it back, young
        Master Thomas—

THOMAS. *(Mock-dignified.)* You seem to forget that
        I am a baronet and the oldest here!

GEORGIANA. The oldest, but who's the wisest?

THOMAS. You know, I've always thought I could be
        a military man. Just think of me in a war outfit.
        With brass buttons. Lots of brass buttons. And
        the other shiny things they put on you.

GEORGIANA. Medals?

THOMAS. And the dangly yellow things on the shoul-
        ders—and, and a sword. A sharp sword to
        match the dagger. And a plume of feathers
        on my hat. All along here, like this! Like the
        Romans used to wear on their helmets.

GEORGIANA. If you want a complete Roman outfit,
        we can probably get you a leather skirt.

THOMAS. Shiny boots! And white gloves! Ah, and
        Miss Jane Fields would be a perfect woman to
        stand by such a noble looking man.

CATHERINE. You can't be serious.

THOMAS. Well, I must say that the gloves would be a
        necessity.

CATHERINE. Not the gloves. Jane Fields.

THOMAS. Why not? Miss Fields is a lovely woman.

CATHERINE. That hyena? She is as loud as a parrot.
        Does is not bother you that just three years ago
        she was a factory girl? It is vulgar.

THOMAS. It is not. She is a sweet girl. She calls me
        Teddy.

CATHERINE. This is what we reap from father's mingling of classes!

THOMAS. Money is a definite attraction, you can't deny that. Her father worked hard in that factory and he worked smart.

CATHERINE. Smart? That donkey?

THOMAS. Are you so obsessed with the animal kingdom?

CATHERINE. Such class jumping ought to be guarded against!

THOMAS. Whatever you may think of Mr. Fields personal manners, he is a mechanical and economic genius. He made himself indispensable.

GEORGIANA. Thomas, are you being serious? This is not one of your larks?

THOMAS. What about me is not serious? Am I painted like some jester with bells and cap? What about me does not appear serious?!

(Pause. GEORGIANA and CATHERINE look at THOMAS, look at each other, and then look away.)

Well, Father would have approved, you know that he would have, Georgiana.

(GEORGIANA gazes at THOMAS momentarily, sincerely considering his statement. She looks back at her Father's portrait, something stirring deep within her. But then, almost coldly:)

GEORGIANA. Papa still understood propriety.

(THOMAS, genuinely surprised by this response, goes to GEORGIANA and takes her by the hands.)

THOMAS. Or, perhaps I understood Father in ways that not even you fathom. Please, Georgie, I would like your approval.

GEORGIANA. You are supposed to head this family now. Why would you need my approval?

THOMAS. Perhaps, but as we have seen, what is supposed to be...

(Presenting GEORGIANA with the dagger)

...and what *is*, are two different things.

GEORGIANA. I do not like Jane Fields, Thomas.

(This visibly hurts THOMAS for the slightest of moments, but then he checks himself and once again puts on the fop.)

THOMAS. Well, la de da, you're always so serious, Georgie! Let us finish our card game—

CATHERINE. Yes, I was winning—

(They begin to sit at the card table. Enter MARY.)

MARY. Miss Georgiana, there is a gentleman here for you. Should I bring him in?

GEORGIANA. Did he leave his name?

MARY. Sir Darrel Fredericks, Mum.

CATHERINE. A great man like Sir Fredericks? And he wants to talk to *Georgiana*?

THOMAS. Did you see not them at the assembly the other night, Catherine?

CATHERINE. No. Was he there?

GEORGIANA. You must have been too caught up with Mr. Johnson to notice. And Mr. James— and Mr. Baker—And Mr. Evanson—

THOMAS. He was paying the most rapt attention to Georgie. Now where in the game were we?

CATHERINE. To Georgiana? But he's so very handsome—very respected—

GEORGIANA. Always so predictably, delightfully
vain, aren't you, Catherine?

CATHERINE. Please, do not get me wrong, dear Georgiana —

GEORGIANA. No, I think I understand you quite
clearly. I told Sir Fredericks the other night
that he was welcome to come to our home any
time he pleased. We run in many of the same
circles — thus he and I are very well acquainted.
Please, see him in, Mary.

MARY. Like a cricket on a skillet, Mum.

(Exit MARY.)

GEORGIANA. Let us see if we can crack into the moti-
vations of a man who would woo a she-troll.

THOMAS. Nonsense, Georgiana.

(Back to the cards.)

Ah, I can't remember where we were--

CATHERINE. I was winning.

GEORGIANA. We'll start the points over and deal
Sir Fredericks in.

CATHERINE. But I was winning!

(Enter MARY with DARREL FREDERICKS.)

MARY. Sir Darrel Fredericks.

(Exit MARY.)

DARREL. Lady Highett!

GEORGIANA. Why, Darrel, it is wonderful to see you
again! I was wondering when you would take
up my invitation. Sit down and play cards with
us. Come, we have placed the table by the windows to take advantage of the warmth of the
sun.

CATHERINE. Yes, it was so chilly this morning!

DARREL. *(Looking out the windows.)* Oh, what a
     beautiful view you have! And those gardens!

GEORGIANA. Come, Darrel, play!

DARREL. What is the game?

ALL THREE HIGHETTS. Hearts.
     (They all sit to play.)

DARREL. A pleasure. Certainly.

GEORGIANA. You will of course call me Georgiana,
     won't you? We have known each other long
     enough. I absolutely detest those wretched
     formalities.

DARREL. Of course.

GEORGIANA. I was just talking about you, Darrel.
     He is quite the accomplished man, you see,
     Catherine.

DARREL. No, no, Georgiana is the one who has im-
     pressed me! A woman of refinement, of feeling.

GEORGIANA. And my beauty?

DARREL. Why, that of a Greek goddess.

GEORGIANA. A Greek goddess! Note that, Cathe-
     rine, a "Greek goddess." Artemis, the chaste
     huntress? Athena, the goddess of wisdom?

DARREL. Aphrodite, the goddess of beauty.

GEORGIANA. You are a detestable liar.

DARREL. Pardon me?

GEORGIANA. *(Laughs.)* I am hardly one of those
     simple women you are accustomed to luring in.
     You are as transparent as water.

DARREL. I do not understand what you mean.

GEORGIANA. Do you deny that you go from wealthy

woman to wealthy woman, trying on each of their estates for size?

CATHERINE. Georgiana, your manners are enough to repel an elephant.

THOMAS. Catherine!

GEORGIANA. Again with the animals—my, oh, my! Well, Catherine, let us see if I can come up with a few animals of my own.

CATHERINE. Look how she has treated this good gentleman here!

GEORGIANA. Sir Fredericks has become as fragile as a humming bird.

DARREL. *(Suddenly, to* CATHERINE.*)* Actually, I actually did not come to see your sister, Miss Catherine. I came to see you.

GEORGIANA. As deceptive as a chameleon.

DARREL. I was hoping that through Georgiana I would meet the fair Catherine who I have heard so much about.

GEORGIANA. And as cunning as a fox.

DARREL. Since I was well acquainted with Georgiana, I was hoping that, through our friendship, she would introduce me to you.

CATHERINE. You came to see me?

GEORGIANA. You must be the most simple woman alive, Catherine.

CATHERINE. I did not know you were the jealous type.

GEORGIANA. Yes, as jealous as if you were dancing with a giant scorpion.

DARREL. Please, Georgiana, enough with the animals!

GEORGIANA. A shrieking owl.

CATHERINE. Someone ought to take those blades out of your mouth.

GEORGIANA. And someone ought to take that champagne out of your brain.

THOMAS. Now come, let us all be reasonable.

CATHERINE. You resent the fact that when I am happily married that you will be an old spinster forever.

GEORGIANA. If you are going to marry the likes of Darrel Fredericks, I doubt you will ever be happy!

DARREL. Marry?

CATHERINE. I am sure Sir Fredericks would make a fine husband.

DARREL. Husband?!

GEORGIANA. I shall not marry because I will not have any man who is not worth having.

CATHERINE. Really, Georgiana, how could you be so rude to poor Sir Fredericks?

DARREL. Poor? Ha!

DARREL. Really, ladies—

GEORGIANA. Most men seem to build up this flittering bird of a woman—a docile, brainless thing of insignificance—

    (Motioning to CATHERINE.*)*

—like this girl. If men desire such a tender beast, I do not find many men worth having.

THOMAS. On behalf of my gender, I am flattered.

GEORGIANA. But do not fret, Darrel. You must understand that I am not so mean spirited as I

seem. I just like a nice battle—for me, it is a
sign of affection. By the way—

(Putting down her cards.)

—the Queen of Spades and all the hearts. I win.

CATHERINE. Drat!

DARREL. *(Disconcerted.)* A risky strategy.

GEORGIANA. You will find, *Darrel*, playing with the
Highetts is not for the weak of heart. We take
our entertainment very seriously.

DARREL. *(Standing.)* You know, I am not very good
at these games of chance.

GEORGIANA. What? Love is not a game of chance?

CATHERINE. Oh please, do not feel compelled to
leave on account of my sister, Sir Fredericks.

GEORGIANA. *(With a smile.)* Yes, I enjoy a good farce.

CATHERINE. Come, I want to show you the new
furnishings in the ballroom—then you must see
the gardens up close!

DARREL. I do not think Georgiana would like me to—

CATHERINE. But I would like you to.

DARREL. Well—all right then.

THOMAS. Let's all go together!

(All look at THOMAS, stupefied.)

THOMAS. As a group, you know, what.

GEORGIANA. *(Dryly.)* I am delighted. Thrilled.
Ecstatic.

*(Exit CATHERINE and DARREL. THOMAS grabs GEOR-
GIANA before she can leave.)*

THOMAS. Behave yourself.

GEORGIANA. I always behave myself.

THOMAS. No, you don't.

GEORGIANA. I cannot help it that she doesn't know when she is being insulted.

THOMAS. She knows *when* she is being insulted, she just does not know *how* she is being insulted.

GEORGIANA. *(Laughs.)* What would I do without you, Thomas?

THOMAS. With Catherine as your sole company? Die of boredom, I suppose.

(THOMAS and GEORGIANA laugh and exit. After some moments, enter MARY with STEPHEN LOCKHART. STEPHEN is a handsome gentleman of the upper classes.)

MARY. My, we're in the mire with visitors today, aren't we? As stuffed as a duck on Christmas, I dare say. Sounds like they're in the ballroom.
(MARY heads towards the ballroom.)

STEPHEN. You don't recognize me, do you, Mary?

MARY. Should I? What did you say your name was again, sir?

STEPHEN. Stephen Lockhart.

MARY. Lockhart—oh my! Little Stevie Lockhart from Edenbridge school!

STEPHEN. Yes, the little school brat! I was wondering when you would catch on.

MARY. Why, you have grown taller, sir—and filled out nicely! Imagine! Those were dramatic times in this household, sir.

STEPHEN. You should have heard the kind of things being bandied about when Georgiana and Catherine were allowed to enroll.

MARY. It made quite the fuss.

STEPHEN. Mister Highett and the schoolmaster called it their "great experiment" — their women's revolution did not last long, however. He died soon after Catherine graduated and those two are still the only females to have graduated from Edenbridge School.

MARY. Do not tell them I told you this, but they used to come home crying.

STEPHEN. Georgiana as well?

MARY. Aye, though her tears were of a furious kind. The poor dears.

STEPHEN. Strange, I cannot imagine Georgie crying. She always showed such a strong face. She took it bravely.

MARY. Oh, she has plenty of pluck, sir. She may rub some the wrong way, but whatever else can be said about her, she has plenty of pluck.

STEPHEN. Oh, this is strange being back. Edenbridge — this lovely piece of paradise! I loved it here. Graduating from Eden's school was like being cast out of the garden.

MARY. Childhood memories run deep, don't they, sir?

STEPHEN. Yes, they do. I am glad to see that you are just as free with the guests as you always were, Mary.

MARY. The Highetts have never been very strict with me about that sort of thing, sir. And the children have all followed old Mr. Highett's ideas that way. Well, Miss Catherine would rather have me behave more traditionally, but she doesn't make too much fuss about it anymore.

(Enter GEORGIANA and DARREL. They are too caught in their argument to notice STEPHEN or MARY at first.)

GEORGIANA. Why do you persist in pursuing my company?

DARREL. Because Catherine and Thomas cannot keep up with my long legs, so I wish to amuse my time with you. How did you say it before? Oh, yes—"I enjoy a good farce."

GEORGIANA. The venom of your mouth would certainly cause the death of anyone, if your lips were not so small and petite.

DARREL. Oh, if you knew what else I have done with these lips, you would be jealous.

GEORGIANA. (A little shocked, but then:) Hardly. The dim witted damsels you court are simply moving, breathing pieces of porcelain with cotton in their heads.

(Enter THOMAS and CATHERINE.)

THOMAS. My, you two *sprint* when you argue!

CATHERINE. Why, who is this, Mary?

MARY. Prepare yourself, Mum. This is Sir Stephen Lockhart, Mum!

GEORGIANA. *(Startled, noticing STEPHEN and MARY for the first time.)* Lockhart? Stephen—can it be?

STEPHEN. It certainly is, Georgie!

(The three Highetts circle STEPHEN for a moment, much like birds of prey, but with the opposite intent. All of them speak simultaneously.)

GEORGIANA. Stephen! Thomas, Catherine, it is Stephen!

THOMAS. Is that really you, old boy? Why I

thought—

CATHERINE. It cannot be—is it really—?

GEORGIANA. Why, I had never dreamed that I may see you again after graduation—I was devastated at the thought—

THOMAS. —you would have been far from here— well, how is that old cricket arm? Do you remember when—?

CATHERINE. I would hope you would forgive me for that time—

GEORGIANA. —but here you are! My confidante, my ally, my childhood friend! Could that possibly be you?

STEPHEN. *(Laughs.)* One at a time, one at a time! I did not die, you know.

(The Highetts make a circle around STEPHEN, *chanting quite enthusiastically in Latin:)*

GEORGIANA, THOMAS, and CATHERINE. Non sans droict, novus ordo seclorum... non sans droict, novus ordo seclorum...

(Stephen joins in:)

...non sans droict, novus ordo seclorum!

(They laugh heartily.)

STEPHEN. Now there is a relic from our childhood!

THOMAS. Why, it is good to see you, chap! A regular prodigal!

CATHERINE. My, oh my, it *is* Stephen. I did not even recognize you. You are—you are quite different now.

STEPHEN. Well, I am taller.

CATHERINE. You did much more than grow taller.

STEPHEN. And you were that little girl who always
        made fun of her older sister's awkward friend.

CATHERINE. I would hope that you would consider
        that I had grown out of that peevish phase.

GEORGIANA. I would not.

CATHERINE. I am much more adult than when you
        last saw me, am I not?

DARREL. *(Clearing his throat.)* Mm-Hm!

CATHERINE. This is — er — yes, Darrel... er, yes, Sir
        Darrel Fredericks.

STEPHEN. Sir Stephen Lockhart. It is a pleasure to
        meet you, sir.

DARREL. If you say so.

GEORGIANA. You are a burst of sunshine in a dark
        time, Stephen.

STEPHEN. Yes, I read about your father's death. That
        is part of the reason that I thought I would
        come. My sincere condolences.

CATHERINE. Yes, Georgiana, he is sunshine! You are
        an absolute beacon, Stephen. I just hope that I
        have become as beautiful as you are handsome.

GEORGIANA. I believe that is the most blatant thing
        I have ever you say, Catherine — and that is say-
        ing a bit. Why, you have embarrassed Stephen.
        Is that not right, Stephen?

STEPHEN. Well —

CATHERINE. Oh stop being a prude, Georgiana. It
        was a perfectly appropriate thing to say.
        Was it not, Stephen?

STEPHEN. I suppose I could say —

GEORGIANA. Do not feel compelled to answer that,

Stephen. Well, Catherine, Darrel has come to
see you and Stephen has come to see me—

CATHERINE. But—

GEORGIANA. Thus, you and Thomas can show
Darrel around the gardens, while I catch up
with my dear friend.

CATHERINE. Oh, but—

DARREL. Yes, for once I agree with your sister.

(DARREL *takes* CATHERINE *by the arm and the two exit
along with* THOMAS. *Exit* MARY.)

GEORGIANA. Well, Stephen, you have changed, my
friend!

STEPHEN. Have I?

GEORGIANA. Why, where is the ungainly, fumbling
friend of mine? Where are his tousled hair and
freckles? Where is my awkward, little, rich
boy? All I see before me is a confident, polished
gentleman.

STEPHEN. And you Georgie! I am hearing all sorts of
rumors!

GEORGIANA. It's rot—do not believe a word of it.

STEPHEN. But I do believe it. I knew you would turn
into something impressive.

GEORGIANA. I am hardly something impressive.

STEPHEN. You were always something impressive. I
am sure your father was very pleased.

(STEPHEN *pauses, seeing the pain cross* GEORGIANA)
What a blow that must have been.

GEORGIANA. The ache is beginning to recede. It was
unexpected, but those last few days with him—
he tried to instill strength in us. He wanted us

to keep rising higher. Rising Highett. Thus, the best way to comfort me at this time, is not to dwell upon it. Especially with you here. Give me a way to serve you. Is there anything I can help you with?

STEPHEN. Can I be honest?

GEORGIANA. Hello, Honest.

STEPHEN. I will be frank then.

GEORGIANA. Hello, Frank.

STEPHEN. Oh, our childhood games! I had almost forgotten.

GEORGIANA. I never forgot.

STEPHEN. Oh, it is a joy to be with you again, Georgie — but I must admit, I had planned this trip even before I heard about your father. There is actually something I need assistance with. I heard that you could help me.

GEORGIANA. In what way?

STEPHEN. Do you remember my ambitions to be a writer?

GEORGIANA. Yes, I thought they were foolish notions at the time.

STEPHEN. I have finished something decent, Georgiana. Much more than decent actually. I dare say it is rather good! A periodical, a drama!

GEORGIANA. What is it about?

STEPHEN. Honor! Terror! Oppression! Revenge!

GEORGIANA. Amusing. You must let me read it.

STEPHEN. Oh, Georgie, how do I ask you this? I hear that you have become very influential. You are not far from London here and they say you go to your home in the city quite a bit—people say that you know people and that people know you. People like publishers.

GEORGIANA. I see.

>(*Pause, disappointed, but then recovering:*)

I am sure that I can find someone to take a look at it.

STEPHEN. Truly?

GEORGIANA. Publishers, publishers. I know quite a few, but which would be most suitable?

GEORGIANA. Mr. Johnson, perhaps? No, on second thought, I would not suggest him—why, of course! Our family knows a fine editor named Harold Lowe who was dear friend of my father's. Oh, if you had only been here earlier, he came by.

STEPHEN. Truly?

GEORGIANA. (*Looking at Stephen squarely, having a sudden thought.*) Stephen—I wonder—

STEPHEN. What is it?

GEORGIANA. Hm. I think I know how I want to do this—why should we not make a fine time of it?

STEPHEN. What do you mean?

GEORGIANA. Do you dance better than you used to?

STEPHEN. I always danced well!

GEORGIANA. Hm?

STEPHEN. Well—for someone my age I danced re-markably.

GEORGIANA. Hm?

STEPHEN. Ah, blast it all, Georgie! Yes, I dance better

than I used to.

GEORGIANA. Good, because Harold's family loves assemblies, parties, balls and the like. If I were to host one here and begged his presence — why, I am sure he would come.

STEPHEN. Oh, Georgiana, that is a wonderful idea! I knew I could count on your sharp mind. You always did impress me.

GEORGIANA. I did?

STEPHEN. There was no person in that school — boy or girl — more intelligent than you. There was no one so witty as you.

GEORGIANA. And you favored that?

STEPHEN. Why else would have I spent so much time with you?

GEORGIANA. I thought that we outcasts just naturally came together.

STEPHEN. But we are outcasts no longer.

GEORGIANA. You surprise me, Stephen.

STEPHEN. Why so?

GEORGIANA. I see you so differently now. You — have changed.

STEPHEN. How so?

GEORGIANA. You seem to have more — never mind.

STEPHEN. Ah, always the sphinx, aren't you? Very well, keep your secrets. I will discover them someday.

GEORGIANA. I assure you, it will be quite the remarkable man to learn the secrets I hold.

STEPHEN. And you do not think that I am up to the challenge?

GEORGIANA. Perhaps you are.

STEPHEN. Well, this Oedipus will have to solve your riddles another day then, for I am afraid I must leave you early.

GEORGIANA. So soon?

STEPHEN. There is some business I have to attend to in the area, but I shall be back before the end of the day, manuscript in hand. Then we can really talk like we used to. I will find Mary to see me out.

GEORGIANA. Do not bother, she is right behind the door. Is that not right, Mary?

(Enter MARY.)

MARY. I was just polishing the silver, Mum.

GEORGIANA. Mary loves a good bit of gossip. She has an ear that is shaped well for key holes.

MARY. Innocent as a lamb in the butter, Mum.

STEPHEN. I do not think I understand your analogy, Mary.

MARY. Oh, there is a kind of wisdom that comes with age that nobody else seems to quite understand.

STEPHEN. I—I see.

(Back to GEORGIANA.)

Well, thank you again.

GEORGIANA. The pleasure is mine. I look forward to seeing you tonight.

STEPHEN. Goodbye then, dear friend.

(MARY and STEPHEN exit. GEORGIANA twirls and drops herself on a couch, with what sounds like a surprisingly girlish giggle. Blackout.)

Margie Johnson as Georgiana Highett and Brandon West as Thomas Highett. Photo by Randy Seely.

Samuel Schofield as Darrel, Brandon West as Thomas, Margie Johnson as Georgiana, and Amber James as Catherine. Photo by Randy Seely.

Jamie Denison as Georgiana Highett. Photo by Greg Deakins.

Jamie Denison as Georgiana Highett and William Mc-Callister as Stephen Lockhart. Photo by Greg Deakins.

SCENE TWO

Enter DARREL and CATHERINE in riding outfits.

CATHERINE. — and then she said that I had not the
sense to discern a jackal from a labrador. And
she said that the labrador had more intelligence
than I did! She said it much better than that,
though — am I not so cruelly mistreated, Darrel?
DARREL. A regular martyr, my dear.
CATHERINE. Oh, she and Thomas are as thick as
thieves! They have always been like that! And
then there I am left out in the cold. I so wanted
to be like them growing up. To be considered
witty and intelligent — but I could not keep up,
you see. You know what else she dared say?
Why, she blatantly —
DARREL. Sh. Enough talking.
CATHERINE. Oh, But —
DARREL. Really. You are done.
CATHERINE. But —
DARREL. You are exceptionally taking today.
CATHERINE. Truly?
    (*Enter MARY. She gives DARREL a piercing stare.*)
MARY. Ma'am, Jeffrey has finished stripping down
the horses. Is there anything else you wish him
to do with them?
CATHERINE. Uh, no, no. That is quite all right, Mary.
Put them in the stables.
MARY. If you need me, I will be as accessible as a cat

looking for a rat.

CATHERINE. That will not be needed, Mary.

> (*Exit* MARY *with another withering look at* DARREL.)

CATHERINE. So you think I am "taking," even in this outfit?

DARREL. When I saw you on that horse, you looked so elegant and noble. A truly romantic figure.

CATHERINE. Do you truly think so?

DARREL. You know I do. I adore you.

CATHERINE. *(With a discreet smile.)* So you say.

DARREL. I can do much more than say it.

> (DARREL *goes to kiss* CATHERINE. *She pulls away.*)

CATHERINE. What are you doing?

DARREL. I was trying to kiss you.

CATHERINE. I am not cheap, Sir Fredericks.

DARREL. Oh, it is "Sir Fredericks" now?

CATHERINE. Yes, and it will continue to be so until you remember that you are with a lady.

DARREL. *(Laughs.)* You are made of the same metal I am, Catherine. Your marionettes and shadow shows do not fool me. You put on the proper face, which is good. We cannot have anyone suspecting us, can we?

> (DARREL *once again draws in,* CATHERINE *draws back.*)

CATHERINE. I am in earnest, sir.

DARREL. You do not have to pretend with me. I have seen your concealed looks and unblushing thoughts. I attract you and its certainly not because of my virtue. Nor yours.

> (*Enter* MARY *in a rush, with a cart for tea.*)

MARY. Shall I serve tea, Mum?

CATHERINE. Thank you, Mary!

MARY. Would Mr. Fredericks like to continue to be a burden and join you?

DARREL. *(Giving* MARY *an annoyed glance.)* I do not think that is necessary.

MARY. As you wish, sir. Anything to please you, sir. *(Exit* MARY.*)*

DARREL. That maid of yours is quite the snoop.

CATHERINE. Mary? She is harmless.

DARREL. Darling, I consider myself a progressive man. I refuse to tie myself to artificial moralities.

CATHERINE. You think they are artificial?

DARREL. Catherine, you must not be so nervous around me! I have only your best interest — our *mutual* best interest in mind! I only look to our future.

CATHERINE. Our future?

DARREL. You are the dearest of women to me. You have something very — alluring. You are like an exotic spice mixed with the sweetness of cinnamon. Fragrant, almost — narcotic. Like opium. I shall love you to the day I die.
*(*DARREL *goes to exit.)*

CATHERINE. Wait. Mr. Fredericks, I — Darrel —
*(*CATHERINE *walks over to* DARREL, *lifts her head and closes her eyes, offering herself for a innocent kiss.* DARREL *smiles and lunges into a much more passionate kiss than* CATHERINE *had expected. She resists at first, but then melts into it. Enter* MARY.*)*

MARY. My, my, Mum! I'm sorry to interrupt, but —

CATHERINE. *(Jolting away from the kiss.)* Mary!

DARREL. Oh, I swear.

MARY. Oh, but it is most important, sir.

CATHERINE. What is it, Mary?

MARY. I—er—

CATHERINE. What is it?

MARY. I can't tell you in the presence of Mr. Fredericks! It's a very delicate family matter!

DARREL. Very well. Goodbye, dear Catherine.

CATHERINE. Goodbye, Darrel.

    (Exit DARREL.)

CATHERINE. Nothing is wrong, is it, Mary?

MARY. Miss Catherine, your fox has a pleasant appearance to him, such a red haired furry fellow. But you don't trust a fox with chickens. You don't let him near your best birds, Mum.

CATHERINE. Mind your own business, you busy old snoop. For once, know your place!

Amber James as Catherine Highett and Samuel Schofield as Darrel Fredericks. Photo by Randy Seely.

Cabrielle Anderson as Catherine Highett. Photo by Bryn Randall.

SCENE THREE

GEORGIANA is reading a book. She is intent upon its contents, engrossed. THOMAS enters, sneaking up on GEORGIANA from behind. He pounces on her and begins to poke her, giggling mischievously. GEORGIANA laughs as he tickles her.

GEORGIANA. What—oh, stop it, stop it, Thomas!
> *(Laughs, but then slaps away his hands.)*
> I said stop it!

THOMAS. Has some gypsy had you under a trance?

GEORGIANA. What do you mean?

THOMAS. I have been calling you for twenty minutes!

GEORGIANA. You have?

THOMAS. Are you ill?

GEORGIANA. No. No, I am fine.

THOMAS. What is that you have your nose in?

GEORGIANA. Nothing.

THOMAS. Oh, now you do have me intrigued!

GEORGIANA. Really, Thomas, it is nothing of consequence.
> *(THOMAS swipes the book from GEORGIANA.)*

GEORGIANA. Thomas, give that back!

THOMAS. Why, it can't be—

GEORGIANA. At once. Give it back!

THOMAS. What a farce! What a delight!

GEORGIANA. Thomas!

THOMAS. A romance! Has the end of the world finally come? Is this what kept you up so late last night, Georgiana?

GEORGIANA. It is fine literature.

THOMAS. Jane Austen? Never heard of her. But I am sure she is very skillful in telling a maudlin story of swooning maidens.

    (Acting.)

Oh, Reginald! Save me! I am all alone in this big, gothic castle!

GEORGIANA. Do not be childish.

THOMAS. I hardly recognize you, Georgiana. The severe spinster has become sentimental.

(GEORGIANA grabs back the book.)

GEORGIANA. Do not make a fool of yourself. I have read nearly every other book in the house. My options are becoming rather narrow.

THOMAS. Narrow indeed!

GEORGIANA. Put it aside, there is another matter I want to address.

THOMAS. That formal, eh? Out with it.

GEORGIANA. I wish to host a ball here and—

THOMAS. Wait—did you say a ball?

GEORGIANA. Yes, a ball.

THOMAS. Truly, you have been transformed! Catherine, come in here!

GEORGIANA. Oh, Thomas, you traitor, please, do not—

THOMAS. Why? Are you embarrassed?

GEORGIANA. I am no such thing!

THOMAS. Oh, of course not. I don't think that you have been embarrassed your whole life. Completely unruffled. Catherine, come here!

GEORGIANA. Thomas, please, don't make this into

something bigger than it is!

THOMAS. Catherine!

(Enter CATHERINE.)

CATHERINE. What are you off about?

THOMAS. Georgiana wants to host a ball.

CATHERINE. (Peering at GEORGIANA suspiciously.) Thomas, our sister has been replaced with a doppleganger.

GEORGIANA. I have always enjoyed going to balls and assemblies with you, Catherine.

CATHERINE. Yes, to play cards or talk your serious talks. But when have you ever been known to dance at a dance, Georgiana?

GEORGIANA. I know how to dance.

CATHERINE. It is one thing to know how to dance, yet it is a completely different thing to be known to dance. Of course, that may be no fault of your own. One has to be asked first.

THOMAS. That is enough, Catherine. Tell me, do you dispute the idea of a ball?

CATHERINE. Of course not.

THOMAS. Good. I think it is high time! We will prepare the invitations, hire the musicians, prepare some elegant food and have a fine time.

CATHERINE. I have been just aching for something like this. Father's death has been such a foggy darkness!

(They all look to Alexander Highett's portrait.)

THOMAS. Yes. We must pay no disrespect to Father.

GEORGIANA. No, I agree with Catherine for once. Our mourning is over.

(GEORGIANA takes off her black arm band.)

CATHERINE. It is high time!

(CATHERINE, too, tears off her arm band. The two sisters look at THOMAS.)

THOMAS. Father would not want us to grieve forever!

(THOMAS tears off his arm band as well.)

THOMAS. We shall make this the grandest ball that this area has ever seen then! We will need to get you a new dress, Georgiana.

GEORGIANA. I have plenty of dresses.

THOMAS. Yes, they all make you look like a mortician's wife. They are not suitable. That new dress you showed me yesterday, Catherine, where did you get it?

CATHERINE. Well, it is a bit embarrassing, but it was a dingy little shop run by two young women. But the dress was so well made that I decided to buy it anyway.

THOMAS. It is the most beautiful dress I have seen you wear. We will invite the dressmakers here to measure you, Georgiana, they will do splendidly.

GEORGIANA. Thomas—

THOMAS. No arguments, Georgiana. The matter is decided and you have no say in it. Mary!

(Enter MARY.)

MARY. Yes, sir.

THOMAS. I thought you might be listening in, Mary.

MARY. I was just polishing the silver, sir.

THOMAS. Taking that comfortable spot of yours by door while doing so, I am sure. Catherine will

write down some directions for you to a dress
shop.

MARY. Yes, the one on Dover Lane.

THOMAS. Tell the two dressmakers that if they can
come by after with some of their designs that I
will make it worth their while. Give them
instructions how to get here.

MARY. I will be there and back again faster than a
hound after a fox, sir.

(Exit MARY.)

GEORGIANA. Then I shall pay for it. I will not be
babied. Anyway, I do have some sense. I was
planning of purchasing a new dress—I just did
not want to make a big scene out of it.

CATHERINE. Why this will be a treat to see you play
the part of the stylish creature.

GEORGIANA. Now do not think that this will be a
regular thing with me.

CATHERINE. A treat nonetheless. Oh, all the
planning—invitations, musicians, food, silver-
ware, and china! And the guest list—the guest
list—oh, the guest list!

(Exit CATHERINE in a near panic.)

THOMAS. *(Pause.)* So is it Stephen?

GEORGIANA. Pardon me?

THOMAS. Stephen. I am not blind, Georgiana. The
ball, the romance novel—you are behaving
peculiarly, and there is only one thing that I
know that causes that kind of peculiarity.

GEORGIANA. Don't be absurd!

THOMAS. It is not absurd.

GEORGIANA. It is an embarrassing accusation.

THOMAS. It is not a crime to be in love.

GEORGIANA. I'm not!

THOMAS. Look at your behavior.

GEORGIANA. Don't you remember? I am the one who is to never marry.

THOMAS. Oh, dear Georgiana, you are more vulnerable than I thought.

GEORGIANA. Do not mistake this, Thomas, I—

THOMAS. I saw that he came again the other day— and the next—and the next—

GEORGIANA. What is your point?

THOMAS. What was it that he brought with him?

GEORGIANA. His manuscript. He wanted to show me some parts of it.

THOMAS. I see.

GEORGIANA. Truly, Thomas, it is not what you think.

THOMAS. Could it be that someone has truly penetrated your armored heart?

GEORGIANA. How can you—?

THOMAS. Look at me.

GEORGIANA. What?

THOMAS. Look at me.

GEORGIANA. You are treating me like a child.

THOMAS. Look at me. *(She does so.)* Ha! Just what I suspected! You are gone.

GEORGIANA. Gone? Gone where?

THOMAS. Oh, Georgiana, be frank with your brother for once.

(Takes her by the chin and looks again.)

Gone!

GEORGIANA. Thomas!

THOMAS. Gone, gone, gone, gone!

GEORGIANA. Oh, stop being being foolish. How can
I say this in a way that you will understand?

THOMAS. It is not surgery, my dear.

GEORGIANA. Thomas—

THOMAS. Anyone can be wounded by Cupid's arrow
—even you!

GEORGIANA. Thomas, please!

THOMAS. Yes?

*(THOMAS begins investigating GEORGIANA's person in
mildly intrusive ways.)*

GEORGIANA. Thomas—what—what are you doing
now?

THOMAS. Looking for the arrow, of course.

(GEORGIANA pushes THOMAS away.)

GEORGIANA. Thomas, please, be serious! This is
painful!

THOMAS. All right.

*(He takes her by the hands with a mock serious
expression.)*

GEORGIANA. Truly serious!

THOMAS. *(This time sincerely supportive.)* Go on.

GEORGIANA. I must ask you something—something—

THOMAS. Something personal?

GEORGIANA. Yes. Something personal.

THOMAS. Go on.

GEORGIANA. How can I—make myself—more—

THOMAS. Say it.

GEORGIANA. —more attractive to a man?

THOMAS. I never thought I'd hear you say that!

GEORGIANA. I am in earnest. Please, Thomas!

THOMAS. I don't know. How should I know?

GEORGIANA. You are a man, are you not? Tell me what to do.

THOMAS. *(Pause.)* I am really enjoying this moment very much, you know. |

GEORGIANA. Thomas! I—I know it sounds like foolishness—I have always ridiculed it as fool-ishness! But I have never--never wanted to look—well, attractive for a man. I thought I had more dignity than that! But it is—

THOMAS. It is a good move. If you want him as a man, treat him like a man by behaving like a woman.

GEORGIANA. Pardon?

THOMAS. Ornament your hair. Burn your old ward-robe.

GEORGIANA. Remember who you are talking to, Thomas.

THOMAS. Dear Georgiana! There's something hid-den up in you. Something none of us have seen. It is there. Let it out. You just have to help it, that's all.

GEORGIANA. Do you really think so?

THOMAS. Absolutely.

GEORGIANA. But I never expected, if I were to feel such, that I would be—

THOMAS. Yes?

GEORGIANA. Well—

THOMAS. Hm?

GEORGIANA. Frightened. Where does fear play into matters of the heart?

THOMAS. Welcome to your first taste of humility. Celebrate it, my dear.

GEORGIANA. It is ironic. I always thought you the fool of the family, Thomas. Yet you have turned out to be the wisest of us all.

THOMAS. Now do be careful with that. It is our little secret. The disguise of the fool is a convenient device and I am not likely to part with it. *(Blackout.)*

Margie Johnson as Georgiana Highett and Brandon West as Thomas Highett. Photo courtesy of UVU Department of Theatrical Arts.

Jamie Dawn Denison as Georgiana Highett and Derrik Thomas Legler as Thomas Highett. Photo by Greg Deakins.

SCENE FOUR

GEORGIANA with the two dress makers, ESTHER and HANNAH WHITEFIELD. The two dressmakers are both pretty, ESTHER more distinctively than HANNAH, but they both have the appearances of the laboring class. They have brought several dolls and a carrying case.

ESTHER. What is it that you don't like about that
   dress, m'lady? If it is the color—
GEORGIANA. It is not the color. There is too much
   lace.
ESTHER. What if we were to take off the lace up 'ere—
   would that suit you?
GEORGIANA. No, it just will not do. I will not be
   made up like one of these dolls, you under-
   stand. I do have some dignity.
ESTHER. That I can see, m'lady. Of course, m'lady.
   Hannah bring over the one in green. Now this
   one is bit plainer, but—
GEORGIANA. Yes, it is plainer. Too plain. Some-
   thing else.
ESTHER. Yes, of course. Hannah, the one with the
   train—
GEORGIANA. Oh no, that one is an abomination!
ESTHER. The one next to it then.
   (*HANNAH brings over one of the models and GEOR-
   GIANA circles it, inspecting it closely. The dressmak-
   ers note her thoughtfulness hopefully.*)
GEORGIANA. Certainly not.

ESTHER. Yes, of course. 'Ere are two more. Bring them both over, Hannah.

(HANNAH brings over the two remaining dolls. GEORGIANA, again, inspects them, deliberating between the two.)

GEORGIANA. That one is unbearable, but that one—I like that one.

HANNAH. Exc'llent choice, m'lady.

GEORGIANA. But the colors are terrible. Can you change the red and green to purple and green?

ESTHER. Yes, m'lady.

GEORGIANA. I should hope so.

ESTHER. Now, if we can measure you, Miss Highett. Hannah, will you please get out the measuring equipment?

(Enter MARY.)

MARY. Sir Lockhart is here to see you, Miss Georgiana.

(STEPHEN enters, barging in.)

STEPHEN. Hello! Sorry to barge in, but I'm barging in!

(STEPHEN laughs. Exit MARY.)

GEORGIANA. Stephen! Oh! I wasn't expecting you for another hour.

STEPHEN. Yes, I did not intend to be so early. Mary tried to stop me, but that only intrigued me more. I thought I may finally be able to solve one of the cultish riddles of womanhood, if it was that clandestine!

(Noting the dolls.)

Why, I will be stumped. Are you buying gifts

for children?

GEORGIANA. Well, not exactly. I—perhaps it is best
to say—how can I—

(Enter CATHERINE.*)*

CATHERINE. Stephen! I thought I heard your voice
and here you are!

GEORGIANA. It is for Catherine! Yes, these are
dressmakers who have come to show me the
designs for a birthday present I am having
made for her!

(To CATHERINE.*)*

Sorry to spoil the surprise for you, my dear.

CATHERINE. A birthday present for me?

GEORGIANA. Why, of course, dear sister. Come over
here and we will have these two take your mea-
surements.

CATHERINE. Why, I think I have harshly misjudged
you, Georgiana. You are a dear sister indeed.
For you to remember my birthday! And for
you to think of such a thoughtful way to ex-
press your affections and apologies and adora-
tion and—

GEORGIANA. *(Out of* STEPHEN'S *hearing.)* Be quiet,
Catherine. Don't you know that your birthday
is not for another six months?

CATHERINE. Well, yes, but I do not mind. You do not
even have to wait to give it to me.

GEORGIANA. The dress is not for you. I do not want
Stephen to know it is mine until the ball.

CATHERINE. Oh—but I was so looking forward to a
new dress!

GEORGIANA. *(To the dressmakers:)* Well, my dears,
now that Catherine is in on our little *secret*, you
might as well measure her.

ESTHER. We understand, Mum.

CATHERINE. *(Conspiratorially to the dressmakers:)* Fret
not, my darlings, I will make it worth your
while. If Georgiana has not the sense to get me
a new dress, I will just have to take matters into
my own hands.

HANNAH. Thank you, Miss!

> *(CATHERINE, ESTHER, and HANNAH step into a side
> room, from which they can still be heard and vice
> versa.)*

GEORGIANA. *(Back to STEPHEN.)* Now, before we get
to your periodical...

> *(Bringing him to the dolls.)*

...tell me what you think of these.

STEPHEN. Very pretty dolls. Let us see —

GEORGIANA. No, no, the dresses.

STEPHEN. Ah, yes.

GEORGIANA. Which one is your favorite?

CATHERINE. *(From the other room.)* I like the blue and
yellow one.

GEORGIANA. Of course, the most gaudy. This
does not concern you, Catherine.

GEORGIANA. So which would be your choice?

> *(STEPHEN circles the dolls, inspecting them.)*

STEPHEN. This one! With the lace.

GEORGIANA. That one?

STEPHEN. Yes. It is modest, but has an innate grace
in its design. It is a beautiful piece of crafts-

manship.

ESTHER and HANNAH. *(Offstage, from the other room.)*
Thank you, sir!

GEORGIANA. *(Darts an annoyed look, then back to
STEPHEN.)* We really need thicker walls in this
part of the house. Now, there are others. What
do you think of this one?

STEPHEN. It is rather, uhm, severe.

GEORGIANA. Severe?

STEPHEN. Yes. Where is its elegance and softness?
Where is its beauty?

GEORGIANA. It has strength.

STEPHEN. Strong? This is for Catherine, is it not? She
is a pretty girl, she should have a pretty dress.

GEORGIANA. I do not think that even Catherine
should be so debased.

STEPHEN. Georgiana, there are certain things men
and women do simply to please each other.
There is no pride in it—it is a humble submis-
sion to each other's feelings.
*(CATHERINE, ESTHER, and HANNAH have finished and
have now re-entered.)*

CATHERINE. I adore being measured. It always
means something is coming.
(Enter MARY with DARREL.)

MARY. Mr. Fredericks, Mum.

DARREL. Ah, Good evening, beautiful Miss Cather-
ine. Good evening, frightful Miss Georgiana.
(Picking up one of the dolls, amused.)
Revisiting your childhood?

GEORGIANA. Why, do you want to play dolls with

me?

DARREL. And are these two young girls your playmates? Rather rough additions to your social
circle, if you ask me.

GEORGIANA. My relationship is purely professional
with these two. They are making m — er, Catherine a dress for a ball we are having.

DARREL. Yes, I am sure that Catherine has told you
that I will be attending.

GEORGIANA. That is quite all right. I will not notice
you. We will seat you behind the orchestra.

DARREL. 'Tis true, you are no respecter of persons.
You will shuffle me off, as you have your mea-
ger playmates.

(Enter THOMAS, *ecstatically, almost as if he were in
an insane daze, making wild movements and ges-
tures, his voice rising and falling in a frenzied
pitch.)*

THOMAS. Repent, repent, repent! Ye wicked sinners,
ye vile men and women of Babylon, know ye
not that the day shall come when the earth shall
shake to and fro like a drunken man? This very
house shall topple upon us! Repent, repent,
repent!

DARREL. What on earth?

GEORGIANA. What sort of bizarre thing have you got
yourself involved in now?

THOMAS. Today I got religion!

(Laughs.)

It was most entertaining. I'll show you! Mary?

(Enter MARY.*)*

MARY. Yes, sir?

THOMAS. Can you bring in the gentlemen at the
        door, please?

MARY. Yes, sir.
        (Exit MARY.)

GEORGIANA. You did *not*—

THOMAS. I brought the religion home with me.
        (Enter MARY with BRIGHAM YOUNG and JOHN TAYLOR.)

THOMAS. My dear friends and family, we have
        apostles in our midst! Welcome Elders
        Brigham Young and John Taylor! They are
        preachers from America! They followed me
        home—can I keep them?
        (There is a shocked pause.)

GEORGIANA. This must be a joke.

THOMAS. Well, I admit, I think it is rather a novel
        treat, but I think you will find them very
        serious. Mormons! Latter-day Saints is what
        they call themselves. I just stumbled upon
        them, really, and opened them like Pandora's
        box!

JOHN. Not so much like Pandora's box, sir. We have
        something much better to give the world. We
        have the truth.

STEPHEN. The truth!
        (Laughs.)
        He has the truth! And I am sure he will sell it to
        us at a discount.

THOMAS. I was just walking absent mindedly
        through Liverpool and I heard this man's...
        (Motioning to BRIGHAM:)

...strong accent. I stopped to discover a whole group had gathered to hear him preach about Jesus, oh, and angels and scripture and fa-la-la! Afterwards, if you can imagine, they told me to repent and be baptized right where I stood! Without any water in sight! We had a pleasant talk anyway, and I even bought a book off them.

GEORGIANA. That still does not explain why you brought them here.

THOMAS. I told them that, if they were brave enough, they could have a whole house of infidels to preach to. And here you all are!

CATHERINE. *(Mortified:)* It is like the '38 Christmas ball all over again.

THOMAS. Introductions: therse are my two lovely sisters, Ladies Georgiana and Catherine Highett, and this is Sir Stephen Lockhart, and then Sir Darrel Fredericks.

BRIGHAM. Nice to meet you, folks.

(BRIGHAM sticks out his hand, but no one receives it. JOHN bows, knowing the protocol.)

JOHN. It is our pleasure to make the acquaintance of such distinguished persons.

CATHERINE. You are not an American like your companion, Elder Taylor.

JOHN. Unlike Elder Young, I was born in England, but have since lived in Canada and then the United States. But who are these two young ladies?

CATHERINE. Do not fret yourself, Mr. Taylor. They

are just a couple of dressmakers.

JOHN. Dressmakers have names, do they not?

> (*To* ESTHER *and* HANNAH:)

I am John Taylor.

HANNAH. Yes, gov'nor. I'm Hannah Whitefield.
This is my sister Esther.

JOHN. Miss Esther, Miss Hannah, it is our honor.

BRIGHAM. (*To* MARY:) And who are you, ma'am?

MARY. Just one of the servants, sir.

BRIGHAM. Why, what a coincidence, I'm a servant
myself. I serve God.

MARY. Well then, sir, you might then say that I serve
Mammon.

BRIGHAM. It is not too late to switch sides, you know.

MARY. Mary, sir. I'm Mary.

CATHERINE. Excuse me, gentlemen, but is it some
strange American custom to mingle with the
hired help while neglecting your hosts?

GEORGIANA. It does not surprise me that religion
does so well over there in your rough country,
Elder Young. Why, the ignorant are always
looking for another barrel to keep their superstitions afloat. Intelligence, science, and noble
philosophy are expected in England.

JOHN. Philosophy? Fried froth.

GEORGIANA. Pardon me?

JOHN. In Paris they have a sort of exceedingly light
cake. It is so light that you could blow it away.
You could eat all day of it, and never be satis-
fied. Somebody asked me what the name of it
was. I said, I do not know the proper name,

but in the absence of one, I can give it one—I
call it fried froth, or the philosophies of men.

GEORGIANA. Oh, and you are so substantial?

BRIGHAM. Ma'am, we carry God's truth restored! We
have a story of new revelation, of an angel
coming to—

THOMAS. (Trying to usher them out now.) Yes, yes,
thank you very much! But now it is time—

HANNAH. Did he say angel?

GEORGIANA. *(Wryly noting Hannah's response.)*
Gentlemen, the converts you will make will be
nothing but the ignorant and poor of England.

BRIGHAM. Rich or poor, doesn't matter much to us,
ma'am. I've been poor all my life.

GEORGIANA. Well then, you will do us a favor if you
can export them all out of here into your own
country. If they are not discerning enough to
see through you, they certainly will not do us
much good here.

DARREL. Now wait a minute, Georgiana.

GEORGIANA. You of all people cannot possibly be
defending these Bible wailers, Mr. Fredericks!

DARREL. Please, I have something to say. Unlike the
rest of you, I have spent some time with these
men and their associates, but more importantly,
time among the class of people they convert—
the class of people you have so degraded.

GEORGIANA. Am I incorrect in my estimations of
their ignorance?

DARREL. Whatever your prejudices about laborers
are, these people are supporting us. They are

the ones making our bread, they are the ones
building our homes, they are the ones building
our carriages. Men and women like Mary here
and the Dressmakers are the ones who literally
make the clothes on our backs. If they will go
to America and build the Latter-day Saints into
a great nation, we would molder and rot. Can
you make a dress? Can you forge a horseshoe
or cook a feast? Without these "lower" classes,
Georgiana, what are you good for?
*(Stunned by the direct insult, everyone looks to
GEORGIANA to see how she will respond. GEORGIANA
coolly regards DARREL and then looks away from him,
as if he hardly mattered at all. She then addresses
the two missionaries.)*

GEORGIANA. I would like to thank Thomas's guests
for coming, but we shall not detain them any
longer.

JOHN. Well, thank you for your time, I suppose.

BRIGHAM. I told ya how this would turn out, Prince
John. Can't trust these uppity types.
(Exit MARY, JOHN, and BRIGHAM.)

DARREL. *(Refusing to be ignored.)* What, no rebuttal?

GEORGIANA. I am done entertaining your forked
tongue, sir. Mary, please see these good minis-
ters back to the carriage and instruct the driver
that they are to go anywhere they please as
long as it is away from here. Stephen, come
with us. Thomas wanted to play some cricket.

THOMAS. Come, Darrel. You will be impressed
with Georgiana's cricket arm.

DARREL. *Georgiana's* cricket arm?

> (*Exit* GEORGIANA, STEPHEN, THOMAS, CATHERINE, *and* DARREL.)

ESTHER. I think they forgot about us.

HANNAH. We can still catch them.

ESTHER. Catch who?

HANNAH. Elders Young and Taylor.

ESTHER. What?

HANNAH. Weren't you interested in what they were saying?

ESTHER. Of course not.

HANNAH. Well, I was.

ESTHER. Don't be daft.

HANNAH. It's not daft. We have to hurry before they get on that carriage!

> (*Exit* HANNAH.)

ESTHER. 'ow are we even related?

Margie Johnson, Aaron Willden, Sam Schofield, Amber James, Fallon Hanson, Tatum Langton, Brandon West and Russ Bennett. Photo by Randy Seely.

Heather McGregor as Hannah Whitefield and McKenzie Steele Foster as Esther Whitefield. Photo by Bryn Dalton Randall.

Debra L. Woods as Mary, Sarah Stewart as Georgiana Highett, Kevin O'Keefe as Thomas Highett, and Cabrielle Anderson as Catherine Highett. Photo by Bryn Dalton Randall.

SCENE FIVE

DARREL and CATHERINE are in a passionate kiss. CATHERINE tries to extricate herself.

CATHERINE. Darrel—
>   (*DARREL continues.*)

CATHERINE. Darrel, give me a chance to breathe!

DARR EL. Come now, this is nothing new to you.

CATHERINE. But right here in the open—where anyone can see!

DARREL. Ah, gentle Catherine—has Georgiana been telling you how much of a villain I am?

CATHERINE. How can I trust you, Darrel?

DARREL. How can you trust anybody? There is a point when you simply have faith.

CATHERINE. Oh, you have taken up religion, have you?

DARREL. I preach a different kind of sermon than they do.

CATHERINE. (*With a smile.*) You're wicked.

DARREL. And so are you, but you look good in it.

CATHERINE. You charmer.

DARREL. Once I started to investigate your family, then I understood what a rare treasure you all were.

CATHERINE. I thought you first were drawn to me as an individual?

DARREL. So I was. Yet, I always make sure I know where I am standing, darling.

CATHERINE. And what did you find?

DARREL. More than you can imagine.

CATHERINE. I do not understand.

DARREL. All in good time, my dear.

> (*DARREL and CATHERINE once again kiss, but then they hear voices approaching. They both stop and listen to them coming closer.*)

CATHERINE. Oh, I am sure to get another scolding for being with you alone.

DARREL. Shh.

> (*DARREL abruptly takes CATHERINE by the hand and they hide behind a couch in a far corner. Enter GEORGIANA, STEPHEN, MARY, ESTHER, and HANNAH.*)

GEORGIANA. I had forgotten all about the fitting that you had with—Catherine today. I hardly know where she could be. Stephen can you stay here, while we look for Catherine?

STEPHEN. Oh, I can help you look, I am sure.

GEORGIANA. No! No. Catherine may come in here and I will need someone to stay while I look through the estate outside.

> (*To the dressmakers.*)

Which one of you has the measuring tools?

HANNAH. (*Holding up her bag.*) I do.

GEORGIANA. Then you come with me in case we find Catherine—so we can measure her immediately.

HANNAH. I understand, m'lady.

GEORGIANA. Come then.

> (*Exit GEORGIANA and HANNAH.*)

STEPHEN. That was strange.

MARY. Pardon me, sir, I really am quite busy. Miss
Whitefield, come with me, please, and I'll
situate you in a different—

STEPHEN. Oh, you can leave her in here, Mary.

MARY. Are you sure that's wise, sir?

STEPHEN. What, are you afraid something is going to
happen?

MARY.   Foxes and chickens—

STEPHEN. Pardon me?

MARY. Barnyard thoughts, sir. I'll be about my
business.

(Exit MARY.)

ESTHER. So 'ave you told 'er?

STEPHEN. About what?

ESTHER. Our little scrap in the street.

STEPHEN. I happened upon your little street meeting with Mr. Young and Mr. Taylor quite by
chance.

ESTHER. My sister's taken a keen interest in them,
'eaven knows why. But the way you badgered
'er and—

STEPHEN. Tosh. Our little debate was hardly of
enough consequence to bring up to anyone.

ESTHER. We're nothin' of cons'quence, are we, sir?

STEPHEN. I did not say that.

ESTHER. But you meant it.

STEPHEN. We just inhabit different worlds.

ESTHER. No, Mr. Lock'art, we in'abit the same world.
The same cont'nent, the same country, the same
city even. And at this very moment, to both of
our discomfortures, we're even in'abit the same

room.

STEPHEN. Miss Whitefield, please—

ESTHER. Sir, you're a writer, aren't you?

STEPHEN. Why, do you think you have read my books?

ESTHER. I—I can't read.

STEPHEN. *(Laughs.)* Yes, that would make it quite difficult!

ESTHER. Please, sir, don't make fun o' me.

STEPHEN. I am sorry. I believe you were trying to drive a point, weren't you?

ESTHER. What do you write about?

STEPHEN. Why?

ESTHER. Nothin'.

STEPHEN. You can speak your mind.

ESTHER. Because—because writers get into peoples 'eads, sir. That can be a good or bad thing.

STEPHEN. You are afraid that I will corrupt everyone, are you?

ESTHER. Sir, the other day you said that we were only talkin' to Mister Taylor and Mister Young because we were poor. Why?

STEPHEN. People of a—well, people in your station are much more likely to try to reach for religion, while people in my station much more readily recognize the manipulation those preachers put upon others. We are in a higher class for a reason.

ESTHER. Why? 'Cause you were born there?

STEPHEN. No, because we stay there. Certain conditions of living create a certain kind of indi-

vidual. In your realms of society there are
thieves, there are murderers, there are drunks
and, if I may be indelicate, there are ladies of
the night. The morals of your people bring
down society.

ESTHER. Sir—per'aps you 'aven't been 'mong my
kind o' people much—but recently, I 'ave 'ad a
chance to be 'mong yours. And you know what
I find?

STEPHEN. Let me guess, you think we are all "snobs."
Posh, eh?

ESTHER. No, sir, that is not what I was goin' to say. I
wasn't goin' to say that at all. I was goin' to
say that I found some very lovely people. I
found that being among a diff'rent people helps
you understand them. You should judge a
person, sir, by the choices they have put before
them, not the choices that they don't.

STEPHEN. Why, Miss Whitefield, that was a nice turn
of phrase. Have you ever thought of going into
forensics?

ESTHER. I'm not that kind o' girl, sir!

STEPHEN. Oh no, you do not understand what I
mean. You have a sharper mind than I gave
you credit for. You know, I enjoy talking to
you.

ESTHER. Why, sir, is that a compliment?

STEPHEN. You earned it. You have impressed me,
Miss—

ESTHER. Whitefield. Esther Whitefield.

STEPHEN. Miss Whitefield. Why—this may sound

strange, but can I see you again?

ESTHER. Me, sir?

STEPHEN. *(Taking* ESTHER *by the hands.)* Why, yes. I
have enjoyed our talk—I would enjoy another.

ESTHER. Truly? Why—I don't know, sir, that would
be nice, I guess. Very nice.
*(The two stand in silence for several moments, and
as they gaze at each other, there is an electric moment.* MARY *enters in a rush.)*

MARY. Oh my.

STEPHEN. Mary!

MARY. Excuse me, sir!

STEPHEN. Were you not supposed to be busy doing
something?

MARY. I was polishing the silver!

STEPHEN. Blast it all, Mary! Why don't you—?

MARY. Miss Georgiana is coming, so you two better
look less—comfortable with each other.
*(*STEPHEN *and* ESTHER *realize that they're still holding hands. They drop their hands, create some
distance from each other and try to look "less comfortable." Enter* GEORGIANA *and* HANNAH*.)*

GEORGIANA. I am sorry, Miss Whitefield, but your
sister and I were not able to find Catherine.
You will just have to come another day.

ESTHER. As you wish, m'lady.

GEORGIANA. Good day.
*(*ESTHER *takes* HANNAH *by the hand and the two
scurry out.* MARY *exits behind them.)*

GEORGIANA. Now, Stephen, finally we can discuss
your story. Let us start where we left off, shall

we?

STEPHEN. *(Emerging from a private revelry, as he looked after ESTHER when she left.)* Hm? What is that?

GEORGIANA. We were deep into your story. Your manuscript.

STEPHEN. Oh, yes. That.

GEORGIANA. Now, Stephen, it shows wonderful promise! You have proven yourself rather profound, you know. I especially love your depiction of the lower classes and their surroundings. The filth, the grubbiness, the immorality—why, it is perfectly accurate.

STEPHEN. Now, Georgiana, it still is a rough draft. I am not sure whether I am keeping—

GEORGIANA. Oh, writers dream of such a rough draft! You are well on your way! Mr. Lowe will be so impressed.

STEPHEN. Really, Georgiana, I am not sure if it deserves that kind of praise.

GEORGIANA. Here, are my new notes notes. I have written here that on page 210—

STEPHEN. You know, Georgie, I am not quite in the mood for this today.

GEORGIANA. What do you mean? We have had such good sessions—

STEPHEN. I know, Georgiana, but my mind is elsewhere. Maybe another day.

GEORGIANA. Are you all right?

STEPHEN. Oh, I think so.

GEORGIANA. You do know that you can trust me? If there is anything that I can help with, I am your friend and confidante.

STEPHEN. Yes, I know. But there is a certain matter I
need to think over.

GEORGIANA. Think over?

STEPHEN. A matter of the heart.

GEORGIANA. *(Caught off guard.)* Truly?

STEPHEN. I have grown — very — well, how would I
say it at this stage? I have grown very fond of
someone. But I cannot discuss it now. Excuse
me, dear friend.

*(Exit STEPHEN. GEORGIANA looks after him, bewil-
dered and hopeful.)*

GEORGIANA. Could it be?

*(She sits on the couch that CATHERINE and DARREL
have been hiding behind. CATHERINE squeals from
behind it. GEORGIANA jolts up, shrieking in return,
twirling around to look at the couch in confusion.)*

DARREL. *(To CATHERINE.)* You are the model of subtle-
ty and stealth, my dear.

*(DARREL and CATHERINE rise from behind the couch,
revealing themselves.)*

GEORGIANA. What are you two doing back there?

DARREL. Trying not to sneeze.

(DARREL wipes the dust from his clothes.)

GEORGIANA. You spies! You were eavesdropping!

DARREL. Which you ought to be glad of, Georgiana.

CATHERINE. Darrel —

GEORGIANA. What do you mean?

DARREL. There is quite a bit going on under your
own roof that you are not aware of.

CATHERINE. Darrel, don't —

GEORGIANA. What are you concealing, Catherine? Well—out with it!

CATHERINE. It is nothing you need worry about, Georgiana.

DARREL. Believe it or not, your sister is trying to protect your heart.

GEORGIANA. My heart?

DARREL. Yes, I know, popular opinion states that you haven't got one.

CATHERINE. Darrel! You promised!

GEORGIANA. Will you stop this taunting? What kind of libelous rumors are going about that would involve my heart?

DARREL. You know, Georgiana, I am the only true friend you have right now. I am the only one willing to tell you the truth.

GEORGIANA. Good! If you have something to say, then say it. I will have none of your manipulations.

DARREL. Did you not wonder why your dear Sir Lockhart dismissed you so easily just now?

GEORGIANA. He did not—

DARREL. Yes, he did.

GEORGIANA. I am sure that he has his reasons.

DARREL. Yes, he certainly has his reasons. It has a lot to do with that little dressmakers of yours. The very pretty one.

CATHERINE. Darrel!

DARREL. There are certain attractions that blind men even to poverty.

GEORGIANA. What?

CATHERINE. Stephen is an honorable man.

DARREL. Whatever his honor dictates in the matter, the fact still remains that Catherine and I over-heard his declaration of affection.

CATHERINE. Interest.

DARREL. *Affection*. Why, he was absolutely singing the praises of that absolutely stunning, little pauper. Ask Catherine, she will tell you the same thing.

GEORGIANA. Catherine?

CATHERINE. I—I—Darrel!

GEORGIANA. Catherine, just tell me it is not true.

CATHERINE. I wish I could.

GEORGIANA. It cannot be true. I know better of Stephen.

CATHERINE. I am sorry, Georgiana. I truly—

GEORGIANA. It is a lie. What are you plotting?

DARREL. No plot. Just concern.

GEORGIANA. Ha!

DARREL. Georgiana, I know this may be hard to believe, but I am watching out for you in this matter. I view it as a personal point of honor to shield you from harm.

GEORGIANA. What does it matter to me? Stephen is his own man. I never entertained an idea of—

CATHERINE. Georgie—

GEORGIANA. Oh, I see what you are thinking—you were thinking that I dared to dream—how could you think that I could scarcely hope to dream that Stephen and I—to dream that—

CATHERINE. Georgiana, let us talk about this later.

GEORGIANA. Excuse me.

(GEORGIANA *exits, repressing the emotions that are running through her.* CATHERINE *turns on* DARREL.)

CATHERINE. You cruel man!

DARREL. Would have you preferred for me to keep her in ignorance?

CATHERINE. You have never cared a shilling for my sister!

DARREL. Are you so sure of that?

(*This catches* CATHERINE *off guard.*)

CATHERINE. Who are you?

DARREL. Who are *you*?

(CATHERINE *exits the room, desperately confused.* DARREL, *somber, walks to a window and looks out at the Highetts garden, as if he desires to take solace from them. Blackout.*)

Cabrielle Anderson as Catherine Highett and Wes Tolman as Darrel Fredericks. Photo by Bryn Dalton Randall.

Rebecca Minson as Catherine Highett and Amos Omer
as Darrel Fredericks. Photo by Greg Deakins.

SCENE SIX

GEORGIANA is beneath the portrait of her father, holding the dagger which Mr. Lowe had given her. She is staring up at the portrait, talking to her father.

GEORGIANA. "Keep it sharp. Keep it sharp. Cut off all those that oppose you—slice through all of their defenses—"

> *(MARY enters.)*

MARY. Esther Whitefield is here, Miss Georgiana.

GEORGIANA. Let her in.

MARY. Are you upset Mum?

GEORGIANA. That is none of your business, Mary.

MARY. Yes, Mum.

> *(MARY exits. ESTHER enters. GEORGIANA places back in its case.)*

GEORGIANA. You are late.

ESTHER. I'm sorry, m'lady.

GEORGIANA. Where is your sister?

ESTHER. She's very ill.

GEORGIANA. Well, I will have to do with you then.

ESTHER. We did not expect this kind of emergency.

GEORGIANA. No excuses. Where is my dress?

ESTHER. There's been some delays, m'lady—

GEORGIANA. Delays!

ESTHER. The sickness.

GEORGIANA. If you expect me to pay you more for your time, then you are mistaken. I will not be cheated.

ESTHER. We don't expect more.

GEORGIANA. You simply failed to meet your deadline.

(*MARY enters with* BRIGHAM.)

MARY. Why, look at that, Mum — we have another
visitor!

BRIGHAM. Really I didn't need to —

MARY. Go on, sir.

GEORGIANA. Ha. What foul fate has brought you
to us, Mr. Young? I had hoped not to see you in
my home again. Nothing has been the same
since the curse of your last visit.

BRIGHAM. I was just going to deliver this invitation,
ma'am. I came to invite you and your family to
a meeting we're having.

GEORGIANA. You are an ignorant fool, if you think
that I would attend any of your spiritual
circuses.

MARY. Now try to be kinder, Mum.

ESTHER. A man o' God deserves anybody's respect.

GEORGIANA. Are you contradicting me, dressmaker?

BRIGHAM. You don't have to do this, Sister Esther.

GEORGIANA. Sister Esther? Have you joined with
these religionists, Miss Whitefield?

ESTHER. My sister 'as, but I 'aven't —

GEORGIANA. Well, at least you have some sense.

ESTHER. But —

(*Slight pause. A decisive moment.*)

I believe they're good people and you were
absolutely cruel to them the last time they were
'ere. They 'ave done nothing but good for my

sister since she joined them.

GEORGIANA. You are a fool.

ESTHER. I'm not alone in my foolery, you 'eartless witch.

GEORGIANA. You siren! I will have no more of you, dressmaker! Have your sister bring me my completed dress!

ESTHER. I—I'm sorry. As soon as we—

GEORGIANA. You better have it here within the week, or I will cut your pay into half.

ESTHER. We need that money!

GEORGIANA. Then you better be quick about it.

BRIGHAM. Miss Highett, she has done nothing—

GEORGIANA. Nothing? Perhaps you should know the character of those you spiritually woo, Mr. Young. This young seductress tried to reach past her station into my friend Mr. Stephen Lockhart. Right in this very room! Do you deny it?

ESTHER. It wasn't like that! You must believe me Mr. Young it wasn't like that—

BRIGHAM. I believe you.

ESTHER. 'ow did she even know we talked?

MARY. Oh, don't look at me.

GEORGIANA. Even with all your charms and pretty gazes, you were quite simple to think that Stephen would last on your hooks. Your face and figure may have been cut into a fine gown, but you are still coarse! And rough! And no amount of lace or finery could ever change what you were born into!

BRIGHAM. Truly, is this how a lady should behave?

GEORGIANA. A lady? Who are you, Mr. Young, to take me into account? It is your people who are unwelcome in this nation, it is your people who are as much as outcasts as this wretched, little rag doll. I assure you that you will not increase your popularity by strengthening your ties to the likes of them!

BRIGHAM. Popularity? Miss Highett, if I now had in my possession sufficient money, as you have, I could buy the favor of the publishers of news papers and control their presses; I could make us the most popular people in this nation, though I expect popularity would send us to hell. Miss Whitefield, perhaps it's time we should both leave.

GEORGIANA. Do not come back, Mr. Young. You are not welcome here. Neither of you will ever be tolerated here.

BRIGHAM. Lady Highett!

GEORGIANA. My life has been nothing but a storm and a fury since you have come into my life, Mr. Young. If there is a God, perhaps he is try-ing to tell me something about you and your religion.

BRIGHAM. But what is it that he is trying to say? God extends His hand to you, ma'am, but if you reject it, you reject the only force which will save you from the coming storms.

GEORGIANA. See them out, Mary.

MARY. *(To BRIGHAM and ESTHER.)* I'm sorry about

all of this.

BRIGHAM. God's work is not through in this house.

GEORGIANA. God is not welcome in this house!

>	(*Exit* BRIGHAM *and* ESTHER. DARREL *enters.*)

GEORGIANA. I get rid of one nuisance only to receive
>	another. Do you want to see Catherine, Darrel?

DARREL. I am here to see Thomas.

GEORGIANA. I hope you are not here for what I think
>	you are.

DARREL. I am not.

GEORGIANA. Good. The last thing I need is you as a
>	brother in-law. Mary?

>	(*Enter* MARY.)

MARY. Yes, Mum?

GEORGIANA. Fetch Thomas for Mr. Fredericks.

MARY. So the fox wants a go at the rooster as well
>	then, eh?

DARREL. Just get him, will you?

>	(*Exit* MARY.)

GEORGIANA. So why the sudden interest in male
>	camraderie?

DARREL. It is none of your business.

GEORGIANA. I suppose it is not. But I do not trust
>	you, Darrel. I never have.

DARREL. I learned never to trust anybody years ago,
>	Georgiana. Especially women.

GEORGIANA. Perhaps there is some wisdom in
>	that—especially this woman. Do not trust me,
>	Darrel. Do not trust me at all.

>	(*Enter* THOMAS.)

THOMAS. Hello, Darrel.

GEORGIANA. Goodbye, Darrel.

(*Exit* GEORGIANA.)

THOMAS. How are you, Darrel?

DARREL. As always, Thomas. As always.

THOMAS. I am surprised that you asked to see me.
Do you plan on asking me for my sister's hand
in marriage?

DARREL. Not yet.

THOMAS. (*Laughs.*) I never quite know what to make
of you, Darrel.

DARREL. As it should be.

THOMAS. Cloaked in mystery, our cunning thinker.

DARREL. I know your secrets, Thomas.

THOMAS. Pardon me?

DARREL. I won't small talk, I won't play with you. I
came here with a purpose. Don't play the fool
with me.

THOMAS. I thought it was well understood that it
was no act.

DARREL. Yes, the foppish Thomas Highett. Fool,
clown, and high brow fellow. Who would
have guessedd that he is an embezzler?

(THOMAS *stops cold. His face falls, as he stares
at* DARREL, STUNNED.)

THOMAS. What the devil!

DARREL. I am a businessman, Thomas. I looked into
your assets long ago.

THOMAS. You what?

DARREL. I always know where I am standing. I
found out that your fortune was much more
than your shipping business in Liverpool or

your family inheritance ought to suggest, as
considerable as the returns from those are.

THOMAS. What are you doing looking at — ?!

DARREL. I also found out why you have shown so
much attention to Jane Fields. Her father has
been helping you embezzle money, I presume,
in return for your help in establishing him as a
respectable figure.

THOMAS. That's a serious charge, sir!

DARREL. Yes, it is. And it is a true charge. You
marrying his daughter will lend them some of
that credibility which they have lacked and
in return he has been slowly sucking money
from his company and into your bank coffers.
Am I accurate thus far?

   (Pause.)

Your silence is illuminating.

THOMAS. Look here, what is it that you want?

DARREL. In return for your continual support of my
publishing company, I will turn a blind eye to
the corruption I have seen and will not report it
to the authorities.

THOMAS. So, all of your involvement with my sister
has been a ploy to get at me?

DARREL. I want to be tied to you by blood, Thomas.
I will need your unerring support no matter
which of your sisters I marry.

THOMAS. Did you say *which*?

DARREL. Somehow your sister Catherine has devel-
oped a conscience. It was the last thing I expected. In any case, Georgiana was the one I

was going to try for in the first place—but you
saw how that went.

THOMAS. Why would a man like you prefer—?

DARREL. Oh, the world doesn't understand the value
of a woman like Georgiana—and I'm not only
talking about her excellent mind. These stupid
men gallop like studs after pretty ponies like
Catherine. But I tell you from experience, it is
the plain women who make the most attentive
lovers.

THOMAS. Here now! You are talking about my
sisters!

DARREL. They are always somebody's sisters. Or
daughters, or mothers, or—wives.

> (*DARREL is sincerely disturbed by his own talk for a
> moment. But as quickly as it came, it is gone,
> shrugging off the brief battle with emotion that
> just came across him.*)

I can have my fun with pretty women, surely,
but a wife...

> (*Giving the word "wife" a bitter emphasis*)

...needs to be something else. Georgiana is a
rare species.

THOMAS. And you think that I'll just submit to you?

> (*At this DARREL zeroes in on THOMAS and, with the
> swiftness of a viper, pushes THOMAS against a wall
> and grabs his throat.*)

DARREL. I know what your game is, and I am prepared for it. I have partners in this. You must
understand that there is more than one wolf on
your trail. Tricky, little bastard that you are, yet

do you think your wits can handle my whole pack of professionals?

(*THOMAS struggles against DARREL's strong grip, but DARREL only knocks him back harder.*)

DARREL. Let me hear you say that you understand.

THOMAS. I understand.

(*DARREL loosens his grip and lets THOMAS go. THOMAS falls to the floor, struggling for air, massaging his neck. He looks up resentfully at DARREL.*)

DARREL. Good. I'll be back in the morning to discuss the details. In the meantime, we have a clear understanding.

(*Pause.*)

Do we not?

THOMAS. Yes, we do.

DARREL. Good.

(*Exit DARREL. THOMAS stares him and then turns over a chair violently.*)

THOMAS. Damn!

(*Blackout.*)

END ACT ONE

Derrik Thomas Legler as Thomas Highett. Photo by Greg Deakins.

Amos Omer as Darrel Fredericks. Photo by Greg Deakins.

Samuel Schofield as Darrel Fredericks and Brandon West as Thomas Highett. Courtesy of the UVU Department of Theatrical Arts.

Margie Johnson as Georgiana Highett, Sam Davis as Brigham Young, and Angela Youmans as Mary. Courtesy of the UVU Department of Theatrical Arts.

Act Two

SCENE ONE

A room in the Highett household. GEORGIANA *is in her new dress, as* HANNAH *works on the last touches and ties up the back of the dress.*

GEORGIANA. *(Tersely.)* Are you almost through yet, dressmaker?

HANNAH. Almost, m'lady. Almost.

GEORGIANA. I ought to dock you some pay for finishing it late. What would you think of that?

HANNAH. It is late, I admit.

GEORGIANA. You could not accuse me of not being fair.

HANNAH. No, Miss.

GEORGIANA. I am sure that you will be glad to leave this house anyway. I suppose you curse the day that you came in here.

HANNAH. It's been a blessing.

GEORGIANA. Pardon me?

HANNAH. Nothing but good has happened to me since I came here, m'lady.

GEORGIANA. Good?

HANNAH. Yes. Good.

GEORGIANA. I have heard of optimism, but that is stretching the principle thin, I dare say.

HANNAH. We met Elders Young and Taylor here.

GEORGIANA. Do not mention those names here,
   Dressmaker.

HANNAH. I beg your pardon.
   (Looking over the finished dress.)
   It is done, Miss.

GEORGIANA. Well, let us see it then.
   (HANNAH brings GEORGIANA to the mirror. GEORG-
   IANA is dumbfounded.)

GEORGIANA. Oh my.

HANNAH. Is there anything wrong with it?

GEORGIANA. I can't believe how beautiful I — it is.

HANNAH. If I may say so, m'lady, it suits you.

GEORGIANA. Does it? It is so different than anything
   I have ever worn. I look so — light. Why, you
   have transformed me! You could make even an
   rhinoceros look beautiful.

HANNAH. We changed the dress to fit your natural
   beauties, Miss Highett.

GEORGIANA. Natural beauties?

HANNAH. Yes, Miss.

GEORGIANA. Such as what?

HANNAH. Well, if Miss would allow me —

GEORGIANA. Yes, yes, show me!
   (GEORGIANA sits herself into a chair in front of the
   mirror. HANNAH is hesitant.)
   Well, get to it. I give you permission.

HANNAH. Yes, m'lady.
   (HANNAH steps behind GEORGIANA and lets down
   GEORGIANA's hair.)

GEORGIANA. Be careful now.

HANNAH. Now look at your eyes, m'lady — their

shape, their color—aren't they beautiful? And see this? M'lady's hair. It is very rich and very beautiful. When we picked a shade of color, we made sure it would point out its highlights.

GEORGIANA. Yes, I see that.

HANNAH. If m'lady is agreeable and would pardon me making the suggestion, Miss might want to do a little more with such beautiful hair. Having it tied into that tight bun all the time may not be exactly the effect that Miss would desire on day such as the ball. With your permission, m'lady, may I?

GEORGIANA. Yes.

(HANNAH *begins working on* GEORGIANA'*s hair.*)

HANNAH. Perhaps you could bring it up like this. Or like this. With a hot iron, you could have ringlets on the sides of your face here and here. There is so much that could be done with it, if m'lady desires it and it is agreeable with her.

GEORGIANA. Do you truly think it is beautiful?

HANNAH. I think you're quite beautiful, Miss. If you don't mind me saying so.

GEORGIANA. Poppycock. My face, what can you do for that?

HANNAH. Pardon me saying so, but there's nothing wrong with your face. It's only that—

GEORGIANA. Come then—out with it.

ANNAH. Pardon me for saying—it's not your face. It's your expression.

GEORGIANA. My expression! What do you mean?

HANNAH. When a woman has something to—live

for, a purpose, meaning—then all of the tight-
ness disappears and she becomes more pleasant
to look at. M'lady is very perceptive to see that,
for she has been using it, and she has been
becoming beautiful, yes?

GEORGIANA. Well, you cannot decorate the soul,
Miss Whitefield.

HANNAH. Respectfully, I disagree. A soul can be
refined. Mine has.

GEORGIANA. So you have been refined in what way?

HANNAH. I daresn't say, Miss. This is close to me,
intimate—this is sacred to me. I will only discuss it, if it can remain sacred.

GEORGIANA. All right then, sacred. What do you
have to tell me?

HANNAH. May I speak frankly?

GEORGIANA. Yes.

HANNAH. Miss and I are the same.

GEORGIANA. That's preposterous.

> *(Pause.)*

What do you mean?

HANNAH. In my temperament, I can seem condescending to others.

GEORGIANA. Condescending? Yes, I can see that.

HANNAH. I get so afraid. As if someday everything
will suddenly break. For years I have thought
if I were righteous enough, kind enough, strong
enough, I could prevent that day.

GEORGIANA. What day?

HANNAH. The day when it suddenly all unravels.

GEORGIANA. Unravels.

HANNAH. Torn to shreds.

GEORGIANA. Shreds. How do you prevent that?

HANNAH. I'm not sure.

(Enter THOMAS. THOMAS *sees* GEORGIANA *and is stunned by the change.)*

THOMAS. Georgiana?

GEORGIANA. What is it, Thomas?

THOMAS. Why, you are—

GEORGIANA. Yes?

THOMAS. You are absolutely—you are absolutely beautiful!

GEORGIANA. Thomas, really—

*(*THOMAS *feigns staggering back and falls over a couch or chair.)*

THOMAS. I'm blinded by your beauty! I'm blinded! Honestly, I can't see! Like Saul of Tarsus!

GEORGIANA. *(Annoyed.)* Thomas—

*(*THOMAS *goes to his knees and starts bowing and groveling to* GEORGIANA.*)*

THOMAS. Have mercy on me, Goddess of Beauty!

GEORGIANA. I am not in the mood for your games, Thomas.

THOMAS. Actually, I am being rather serious, dear. You really do look splendid in that dress. But, Stephen is here.

GEORGIANA. What? What is Stephen doing here?

THOMAS. I invited him to go hunting with me. I am sorry, I, uh—forgot that your dressmaker was going to be over.

GEORGIANA. Oh, Thomas, what a stupid thing to do! Let me talk to him before you go off—but, oh, hurry, Thomas, go get Charlotte and Angelina to help me out of this thing.

(*Exit* THOMAS.)

HANNAH. Perhaps I should take my leave—

GEORGIANA. You can get your pay from Mary, Miss Whitefield. I will give you the full price. Plus tell Mary that I am giving you a ten percent bonus for such quality work.

HANNAH. Oh, thank you so very much! We truly needed—

GEORGIANA. Oh, don't be a fool. Go. Go!

HANNAH. Yes, m'lady.

(*Exit* HANNAH.)

Fallon Hanson as Hannah Whitefield and Margie Johnson as Georgiana Highett. Courtesy of the UVU Department of Theatrical Arts.

SCENE TWO

Back in the drawing room. STEPHEN *waits.* Enter HANNAH.

STEPHEN. Oh. Miss Whitefield. I did not know that you were here.

HANNAH. Well, yes. I'm just on my way out, sir.
(*HANNAH goes to leave, STEPHEN calls out and stops her.*)

STEPHEN. Miss Whitefield!

HANNAH. Yes, Mr. Lockhart?

STEPHEN. How is Esther?

HANNAH. My sister is well, thank you.

STEPHEN. Do you suppose she would mind if I paid her a visit this afternoon?

HANNAH. Sir Lockhart—

STEPHEN. She did tell you about the talk that I had with her, did she not?

HANNAH. Yes.

STEPHEN. Then you understand that I expressed— interest to her?

HANNAH. Yes.

STEPHEN. Good. Is today a bad day to visit then?

HANNAH. I think any day is a bad day to visit.

STEPHEN. What do you mean? What are you telling me?

HANNAH. She—she was flattered.

STEPHEN. Flattered?

HANNAH. She told me that if you and I were able to talk today when I came by—she told me to give you her apologies and she hopes that you will have no ill feelings towards her because of her refusal.

STEPHEN. You are in earnest?

HANNAH. Regretfully so.

STEPHEN. But why?

HANNAH. She—she was flattered. But we—she has decided to—Sir Lockhart, you are in no position to honorably make a future with my sister.

STEPHEN. Are you the one who pressed this decision upon her?

HANNAH. We—Esther—she makes her own decisions, I—she—

STEPHEN. What a farce! I suppose this has much more to do with your ignorant superstitions than anything! Well, let your sister know that your religious tyranny has destroyed any chance we may have had at happiness together.

HANNAH. Esther makes her own decisions, she—she happens to desire somebody who would share what is most precious with her. What is most true.

STEPHEN. You know nothing of truth! We all clutch at it, but there is nothing to hold!

(This startles HANNAH. After a shocked pause, she curtsies.)

HANNAH. Good day to you, sir.

(HANNAH turns to leave, but then stops. She gathers her courage and turns back to STEPHEN.)

HANNAH. I may not have your education, but I have experienced things in this religion that would

knock you off your high place, sir! Supernat-
ural things, spectacular things — sacred things.

STEPHEN. And what if another preacher came along
just as schooled in the art of deception? What
then!

HANNAH. Who is the true deceiver here, sir? Elders
Young and Taylor — or you? Or are you just
deceived yourself?

STEPHEN. You do not know what you are talking
about —

HANNAH. Don't I?

STEPHEN. It is not pragmatic. All it does is make you
discontent —

HANNAH. I did not need this religion to be made discontent! And I am a lucky one. I don't have to
go into those factories and risk my hand and
life to a spinning jenny. I don't have to prance
as a strumpet in desperation. I have not been
thrust that low — but I have seen it and smelled
it and heard it!

STEPHEN. Well, that is the way your God planned it.

HANNAH. No, it's the way that man has made it.

STEPHEN. Things are the way they are.

HANNAH. And you benefit.

STEPHEN. I benefit? With my hungry mind and
empty heart? I benefit!

HANNAH. Don't you, sir? While my people work
and slave, your people live off our sweat, you
build upon our foundations, you oppress us for
our labor! While you grow richer and fatter,
with more and more leisure time, we work our

bones raw and dwindle away into specters of
poverty.

STEPHEN. Why, how dare you accuse me of—

HANNAH. Am I not correct, sir?

STEPHEN. No, certainly you are not—you and Esther
must be able to—to—there is every opportunity
to rise from—from—

(Pause.)

Oh dear.

HANNAH. Sir?

STEPHEN. You are right—you are absolutely right

HANNAH. I—I didn't mean to be contrary.

STEPHEN. Oh, yes you did. Thank heaven for that.

HANNAH. Sir—

STEPHEN. Why have hidden yourself, Miss Whitefield?

HANNAH. I beg your pardon?

STEPHEN. I find you to be quite remarkable. Yet only
now have I thought so. You have been so silent
before—now I find your voice to be thrilling.

HANNAH. I'd better go, Mr. Lockhart.

STEPHEN. Wait. Can I see you again?

HANNAH. Mr. Lockhart, truly—

STEPHEN. I have seen something in you!

HANNAH. What you've seen in me is what you saw
in my sister—women who know who they are
what they believe.

STEPHEN. Please—

HANNAH. Sir, you went from Miss Highett, to my
sister and now you speak sweetly to me—what
next? You didn't want them, you don't want

me.

STEPHEN. How could you possibly know what I
	want?

HANNAH. You want a crutch to hold you up.

(*HANNAH picks up her bag and is about to leave.*)

STEPHEN. You've wounded me.

HANNAH. Frankly, sir, you deserved it.

STEPHEN. Such strength—such confidence. Where
	do you get it?

HANNAH. Goodbye, Mr. Lockhart.

STEPHEN. The book—is that the Apostle's book?

(*HANNAH is leaving.*)

	Please! Wait! Thomas said that they gave him a
	book—is that the book?

HANNAH. Yes.

STEPHEN. I like books.

HANNAH. Yes?

STEPHEN. May I borrow your book?

HANNAH. My book?

STEPHEN. You have one in your bag there, don't you?

HANNAH. How did you know?

STEPHEN. I often carry around what I am reading as
	well. It is one of the differences between you
	and your sister. You love to read.

HANNAH. (*Taking out her Book of Mormon.*) Sir, this
	book is precious to me.

STEPHEN. I will return it to you in good condition. I
	promise.

(*HANNAH considers it a moment and then hands
STEPHEN her Book of Mormon.*)

STEPHEN. Thank you, Miss Whitefield.

HANNAH. Don't be too quick to cast it aside as foolishness, sir. Make you sure you understand a thing before you try to condemn it.

(Exit HANNAH. Exit STEPHEN.)

Tatum Langton as Esther Whitefiel and Aaron Wilden as Stephen Lockhart. Courtesy of the UVU Department of Theatrical Arts.

Aaron Wilden as Stephen Lockhart and Fallon Hanson as Hannah Whitefield. Courtesy of UVU Department of Theatrical Arts.

SCENE THREE

GEORGIANA and MARY are together. GEORGIANA is appareled in her new dress and her hair is styled and decorated. She is self-conscious about her appearance, as if she were exposed. Music is playing from the ball room, as the ball is in full sway.

GEORGIANA. Is it hot in in here? I feel it is very hot. I am sure it is even worse in there with all the people.

MARY. Come now, Miss Georgiana, you must go in there. Your guests are all waiting and you look—

GEORGIANA. I can't. I just can't. I don't see why I got this thing together. I forgot how uncomfortable it gets with all of the heat, the odor, the perspiration—

MARY. Sir Lockhart has been asking after you.

GEORGIANA. Of course he has. He needs me to introduce him to Mr. Lowe—who, by the way, has not arrived!

MARY. Miss Georgiana—

GEORGIANA. How would you like it, Mary, if a man only hung about you because you knew some influential people.

MARY. Now you know that's not the case.

GEORGIANA. Do I, Mary? Do I?

MARY. Well, if that's true, then tonight he has something else coming to him. You look splendid, ma'am.

GEORGIANA. You're my servant, Mary. You're paid
to say that.

MARY. That's like making a cat bark. You know that I
have only ever said what I want to.

GEORGIANA. *(Seeing* STEPHEN *approaching.)* Oh, no!
*(*GEORGIANA *turns her back towards* STEPHEN *as he
enters.)*

STEPHEN. Mary, where's Georgiana? I have been
looking for her all evening.
*(*MARY *motions to* GEORGIANA.*)*

GEORGIANA. I am sorry I have left you waiting,
Stephen. I—
*(*GEORGIANA *turns around.)*

STEPHEN. Georgiana—

GEORGIANA. What? What is it?

STEPHEN. Why, you are—Georgiana! You look
lovely.

GEORGIANA. I—I—

STEPHEN. Splendid, smashing—beautiful.

GEORGIANA. I am not either—it is just a new dress.

STEPHEN. It is not the dress. I am humbled to be in
your presence.
*(*STEPHEN *bows.)*

GEORGIANA. Stephen, stop it, this is embarrassing.

STEPHEN. Mary, are you embarrassed?

MARY. No, sir.

STEPHEN. Then you must be the only one who feels
so, Georgiana. If you had looked into the mirror, perhaps you would have felt differently.

GEORGIANA. I—I don't know how to explain myself.

(The music changes.)

STEPHEN. Recognize the music, Georgiana?

GEORGIANA. Why, of course! Graduation! This was
the song in which you asked me to dance. I'm
surprised you remember that.

STEPHEN. Dance with me!

GEORGIANA. Oh, Stephen I just can't go in—

STEPHEN. All right. Then let us dance here.

GEORGIANA. Pardon me?

STEPHEN. We can hear the music. Let us have one
song when we are not bumping into everybody
in those dreadful lines. I want you to myself for
a moment.

*(GEORGIANA simply nods, a kind of sweet
embarrassment coming over her. They start to
dance.)*

STEPHEN. Remember, my uncomfortable suit coat? I
felt so embarrassed.

GEORGIANA. You were adorable. I am the one who
ought to have felt embarrassed.

STEPHEN. I remember that you wore a beautiful
dress.

GEORGIANA. Yes—it was a bit tight.

STEPHEN. I did not notice. I just thought—oh, never
mind.

GEORGIANA. You thought what?

STEPHEN. I remember thinking that you were my
favorite girl in the world.

(Pause.)

Perhaps I should not have told you that just
now.

GEORGIANA. You should have told me it then.

> (*The music stops. They stare at each other for a moment. They kiss and then separate, still staring at each other.* DARREL *and* CATHERINE *enter.*)

DARREL. Have we interrupted a private moment?

STEPHEN. Good evening, Darrel.

DARREL. Georgiana, is that really you?

GEORGIANA. Good evening, Darrel. You look absolutely splendid tonight, Catherine.

CATHERINE. So do you, Georgiana. You look — like a queen.

DARREL. The dance is in the other room, you know.

STEPHEN. Oh, I see that they want our spot, Georgiana. Should we give it to them?

GEORGIANA. Why not? And you truly do look stunning tonight, Catherine. You are certainly at top form.

> (STEPHEN *and* GEORGIANA *exit.* MARY *exits satisfied.*)

CATHERINE. Did you hear that? Georgiana was — she was — kind to me.

DARREL. What did you think of the woman Thomas is escorting around out there?

CATHERINE. Jane Fields? Well —

DARREL. She is a detestable woman. She has no sense of propriety at all.

CATHERINE. If she can make Thomas happy, then she is quite suitable with me.

DARREL. What? You used to detest her — I thought.

CATHERINE. Well, now I don't. I think I am starting to look at people a little differently now.

DARREL. Oh dear, you have become a wretched moralist, haven't you?

(DARREL suddenly gives a start when HAROLD LOWE *is seen in the doorway.)*

CATHERINE. What is wrong, Darrel?

DARREL. What is Harold Lowe doing here?

(DARREL attempts to retreat the room before CATHERINE *stops him.)*

CATHERINE. Do you know each other?

DARREL. I must leave.

CATHERINE. Darrel, wait—

DARREL. I am sorry Catherine, but I will have to quit the ball early.

CATHERINE. Why? We have planned this for weeks.

DARREL. A personal matter, my dear.

(DARREL tries to pass HAROLD, *bur* HAROLD *brings his cane in front of him, blocking* DARREL *for a moment.)*

HAROLD. It has been some time, sir.

DARREL. Get out of my way, old man.

HAROLD. What are you up to these days? The usual?

DARREL. Get out of my way.

HAROLD. Yes, yes, always your "way." That is the important thing. No matter who gets crushed in the meantime.

DARREL. I do not need your lectures.

HAROLD. Yes, yes, avoid the lectures. Avoid the morality. Avoid those voices from the past. Avoid the voice of conscience!

DARREL. Get out of my way!

(DARREL pushes his way through HAROLD *and exits.* HAROLD *comes over to* CATHERINE.)*

CATHERINE. How do you know him?

HAROLD. He wanted to become a partner with me. I
investigated his past and found some very ma-
lignant pieces of information.

CATHERINE. Partner? But he's not a business man.
He's a—he's part of the aristocracy.

HAROLD. He most certainly is not.

CATHERINE. Pardon me?

HAROLD. What has he been telling you?

CATHERINE. Mr. Lowe, you must understand—it is
not official yet, but he and I—

HAROLD. He's been *courting* you? You must be rid of
him. Do not get caught in his snares!

CATHERINE. Mr. Lowe, you are being absolutely—

HAROLD. Catherine, dear, Mr. Fredericks is already
married. He left behind a wife in London—a
wife who is expecting their first child. Even
when he was still with her, he was unfaithful.
At the time he was so steeped in debt because
of his gambling—he disappeared. He must
have come here under a different identity.
*(Catherine absorbs this information in a stunned
silence.)*

CATHERINE. I have been a fool.

HAROLD. I am afraid to cause you pain, my dear, but
I do it to prevent a deeper hurt.

CATHERINE. I have been so stupid. Harold, what
should I—I have been so stupid!

HAROLD. Catherine, how extensive was your relationship with that man?

CATHERINE. How dare you—how dare you accuse
me of that!

HAROLD. *(Pause.)* I have not accused you of anything.

> *(Exit* CATHERINE, *retreating.* HAROLD *looks after her with concern. Enter* GEORGIANA *and* STEPHEN.*)*

GEORGIANA. I thought I saw you come in, Harold!

HAROLD. *(Trying to hide the seriousness of his previous conversation.)* Georgiana, my girl!

GEORGIANA. Harold, I have been waiting all evening for you! I have some very important things I want to bring up to you. But first, this is my friend Sir Stephen Lockhart. He has been wanting to meet you.

STEPHEN. Sir.

HAROLD. A pleasure.

GEORGIANA. I think that you will both benefit from the meeting.

HAROLD. If he has your approval, Georgiana, I am sure we will. So I imagine you have a manuscript you want to show me.

STEPHEN. Am I that transparent?

HAROLD. Sir, I can spot a writer from a mile away.

Angela Youmans as Mary, Aaron Wilden as Stephen, and Margie Johnson as Geogiana. Courtesy of the UVU Department of

SCENE FOUR

Enter THOMAS *and* MARY.

THOMAS. Mary, I do not understand your line of
   questioning.
MARY. All I am trying to say, Sir Thomas, is that I
   think it odd that you spend so much time with
   Sir Fredericks nowadays.
THOMAS. I have no personal friendship with the
   man. We are doing a bit of business together,
   that's all.
MARY. Business?
THOMAS. Yes, business.
MARY. Is that what you call it?
THOMAS. Call what? Why wouldn't it be called busi-
   ness?
MARY. The walls have ears, sir —
THOMAS. — and flies and windows and pictures.
   What are you saying, Mary?
MARY. I overheard your conversation with Sir Fred-
   ericks.
THOMAS. Mary — you were behind the door!
MARY. Polishing the silver, sir. I polish it nearly
   every day. And I know a great deal more than
   you think — things about this family. I know it
   all more intimately than you do, sir — that Darrel Fredericks is not a nice man. Not a nice man
   at all. He's invaded this house in more than
   one way and I won't stand by as he tries to

destroy it.

THOMAS. Mary, you do not understand. I am too
caught up with it now.

MARY. Say that you were at a picnic, sir. Then this
hornet comes upon your food.

THOMAS. Hornet?

MARY. Yes, a pest, an insect, a hornet with spindly
legs, black eyes, and a fearsome sting. Say
this hornet tries to infest your food. Do you
swat him away?

THOMAS. No, because he will sting my hand.

MARY. So what do you do then, sir?

THOMAS. I deputize him, give him a regiment and
send him off to India!

MARY. Seriously, sir, what do you do?

THOMAS. I do not know.

MARY. But say you have a stick, sir. A big stick. So
when this hornet falls upon your food, what do
you do then? Do you smash the hornet and the
food together?

THOMAS. Yes, to save the rest of the food.

MARY. Then, sir, my suggestion about Darrel Fredericks, is to find a stick. A big one.

(A book flies into the room. GEORGIANA is heard.)

GEORGIANA. *(Off stage.)* Romantic rubbish! You make
a woman dissatisfied!

THOMAS. Oh, do you think she is in one of her
moods? Perhaps I should go in and —

MARY. Don't touch the kettle while it's hot, sir.

THOMAS. True wisdom. Is a retreat in order then?

MARY. Aye.

(Exit THOMAS *and* MARY. *Enter* CATHERINE. *She picks up the book.)*

CATHERINE. Georgiana?

(Enter GEORGIANA.*)*

GEORGIANA. What is it, Catherine?

CATHERINE. I am worried about you.

GEORGIANA. No need to worry.

CATHERINE. Something is wrong.

GEORGIANA. Nothing is wrong.

CATHERINE. Something has been wrong since the ball.

GEORGIANA. Do I need to repeat myself? Nothing is wrong.

CATHERINE. You have been watching the windows for days now. You are waiting for him to come.

GEORGIANA. For who to come?

CATHERINE. I may not have your kind of mind, but I'm not stupid.

GEORGIANA. What do you care about it?

CATHERINE. I care about you.

GEORGIANA. Since when?

CATHERINE. Georgie—

GEORGIANA. You are serious...

CATHERINE. How did the ball go? I was so— distracted. But he showed interest, did he not?

GEORGIANA. Yes.

CATHERINE. He expressed that interest?

GEORGIANA. You could say that.

CATHERINE. But since then he hasn't come.

GEORGIANA. He hasn't come. Catherine, is it possible that a man could regard — could have affection for a woman like me?

CATHERINE. Oh, Georgie —

(*Enter* MARY.)

MARY. (*Gleefully.*) Sir Lockhart is here to see you, Mum.

GEORGIANA. Stephen?

MARY. I thought that might cheer up your spirits. I'll bring him right in.

(*Exit* MARY.)

GEORGIANA. Catherine, he has come!

(GEORGIANA *embraces* CATHERINE. *They both laugh. They separate, somewhat embarrassed.*)

GEORGIANA. We haven't done that for some time, have we?

CATHERINE. Good luck, Georgie.

(*Exit* CATHERINE. *Enter* STEPHEN.)

STEPHEN. Good evening, Miss Highett.

GEORGIANA. It's so good to see you, Stephen.

STEPHEN. As it is to see you.

GEORGIANA. I wondered what took so long for you to come by since the ball. What could have possibly detained you for so —

(*Seeing his hesitation.*)

What is wrong?

STEPHEN. I — I do not know what to say.

GEORGIANA. You are so rigid.

STEPHEN. Please, sit. I have something to tell you —

GEORGIANA. Why are you so formal? What is it? Trust me.

STEPHEN. Well — I —

GEORGIANA. Stephen?

STEPHEN. I am trying.

GEORGIANA. You can tell me.

STEPHEN. I—I am leaving.

GEORGIANA. Leaving?

STEPHEN. To America.

GEORGIANA. America? America! Whatever for?
When will you be back?

STEPHEN. I have come to thank you for your friendship, Georgiana. It has meant a great deal to
me all these years and—

GEORGIANA. What is this about?

STEPHEN. It is a personal decision.

GEORGIANA. A personal decision you cannot share
with me?
    (Pause.)
Stephen, I thought—well, after the ball we were
so close—

STEPHEN. I hope that you did not misinterpret—

GEORGIANA. You kissed me.

STEPHEN. Yes, I know—I know. I meant it—I meant
it then.

GEORGIANA. Then?

STEPHEN. It was a mistake. I am sorry.

GEORGIANA. It was not a mistake—

STEPHEN. Yes, it was. I acted rashly. I am deeply
sorry.

GEORGIANA. That is not the sort of thing a woman
wants to hear about her first kiss.

STEPHEN. I feel—I have been tortured with guilt
about the whole thing.

GEORGIANA. Oh, spare me of any prepared speeches you have to ease my—

STEPHEN. I have joined the Latter-day Saints. There. I said it.

GEORGIANA. Oh.

(*She sits.*)

Oh dear. It is about the Dressmaker then.

STEPHEN. No, it is not that.

GEORGIANA. She is a pretty girl.

STEPHEN. I am sincere in my conversion.

GEORGIANA. It is the Dressmaker!

STEPHEN. Do not jump to such a dramatic conclusion!

GEORGIANA. Dramatic? No, a man like you falling for such a girl is absolutely trivial. It is beneath you!

STEPHEN. Georgiana, this has nothing to do with the Dressmakers. And, my poor darling, it has nothing to do with you.

GEORGIANA. Who has it to do with then?

STEPHEN. It has everything to do with me. Me! I—I have been searching, inquiring, but I did not know it. Not really. Yet now—

GEORGIANA. You are a dyed in the wool heathen like I am. Are you foolish enough to abandon your security for the sake of a dressmaker?

STEPHEN. I have already said—

GEORGIANA. Will you abandon the vigor of our friendship for such gutter children?

STEPHEN. Do not make them a part of this. They are women of goodness. Women of gentleness.

GEORGIANA. Women of weakness! Stop creating goddesses out of the delicate, porcelain faced nymphs of the ignorant!

STEPHEN. Georgiana, how can you be so vain? Can't you see that it is the ugliest part of you?

GEORGIANA. Vain? Vain am I? With my face? I am not one of these crystallized corpses of beauty.

STEPHEN. Please—

GEORGIANA. What feminine qualities, what prancing movements, what horrid lace and velvet do I possess to make me vain?

STEPHEN. It is the conceit of your mind, your own self-regard.

GEORGIANA. You are defensive because I have intellect and depth, while these religionists have nothing, but a polished husk! Emotionalism!

STEPEN. Georgie—

GEORGIANA. What, do I threaten you? Do you feel as if I will debunk your manhood?

STEPHEN. Georgiana—

GEORGIANA. Is the mind of an intelligent, sophisticated woman too much for you? Is this dressmaker so much more to your liking because she will bend to you?

STEPHEN. Georgiana! This is not a contest between you and Esther!

GEORGIANA. Then tell me why else you would take this fantastic journey?

STEPHEN. It is true belief. My belief. It sat well with me—there was truth in it.

GEORGIANA. Truth! There is no truth, only ranting

and raving and flinging the name of God about
as if it actually meant something!

STEPHEN. And that is the difference between us. It
does mean something to me, Georgiana. I am
a believer now.

GEORGIANA. Belief? Belief in what? Will you abandon the pinnacle of the world for that wild-
eyed, beast of a nation?

STEPHEN. I was brought up a gentleman, but I have
cultivated the soul of a beggar. This is my decision. I will not be a laborer for this world.
Better to be the servant of God than to be the
slave of social pharisees.

GEORGIANA. Pharisees! Do not be deceived!

STEPHEN. I am not deceived! Georgiana, I do not
need England's social structure to buoy me up.
And I do not need your approval or that of any
man, woman, or devil!

GEORGIANA. Stop it!

> (They both turn away. Pause. They both attempt
> to regain their composure and repress their emo-
> tions.)

You are a convert then?

STEPHEN. Yes.

GEORGIANA. One of the religious faithful?

STEPHEN. Yes.

GEORGIANA. Oh.

> (They look at each other.)

STEPHEN. Georgiana—

GEORGIANA. Your writing? What is to happen with
that?

STEPHEN. It is nothing to me. Now my once vain ambition can give up any hope for a prominent future and not despair about it.

GEORGIANA. Nothing is the same for you anymore? Your writing means nothing, your country means nothing, your society means nothing?

STEPHEN. Not what they once did.

GEORGIANA. And am I nothing as well?

STEPHEN. Oh, Georgiana —

GEORGIANA. I deserve an answer.

STEPHEN. I care for you — deeply. But I cannot stay.

GEORGIANA. Do you love me, Stephen?

STEPHEN. Love — I hardly know what love is.

GEORGIANA. I have changed. I have put on a new dress, a new face —

STEPHEN. I love you, Georgiana, I always have, I think — but not in that sense. It is like with the dressmakers. I admired them. I mistook that for love. They lifted me to a point, and you lifted me even higher, but it is even greater hands that bore the piercing of nails that have truly brought me bravery.

GEORGIANA. So are you here to cut me loose or ask me to go with you?

STEPHEN. What kind of question is that?

GEORGIANA. I — I will not sacrifice my life on your altar! I will not be controlled by the dictates of a man I have never seen nor a god I have never heard.

STEPHEN. I understand. In fact your feelings have simplified the matter for me greatly.

GEORGIANA. Stephen, I would give up everything for you. You are substance, I can hold you in my hands. If you could just abandon this quest of Quixote.

STEPHEN. Our ships are sailing in different directions—we grow more distant every moment.

GEORGIANA. It doesn't have to be this way.

STEPHEN. I came here to say goodbye, Georgiana.

GEORGIANA. Stephen, don't go. I need you.

STEPHEN. And I once thought that I needed you.

GEORGIANA. Then stay.

STEPHEN. No. I can't.

GEORGIANA. Stephen—

STEPHEN. I believe in this, Georgiana. You and I— we are too different.

GEORGIANA. We are the same!

STEPHEN. No. We are not the same. There is a part of me that you have never known, for it is foreign to you—it was foreign to me. Yet I have discovered a piece of it and now I am in search for the rest. There is something that I long for which you have never sought, never understood, never acknowledged.

GEORGIANA. If it is love, I can love—I do—

STEPHEN. That is not it either.

GEORGIANA. Did you hear what I just said?

STEPHEN. Goodbye, Georgiana.

(*STEPHEN exits. GEORGIANA can't hold the emotion any longer and exits.*)

*Jamie Denison as Georgiana Highett and William Mc-
Callister as Stephen Lockhart. Photo by Greg Deakins.*

SCENE FIVE

The Dressmakers' shop and home. HANNAH *and* ESTHER *are packing a trunk. We see that they are very poor and can only maintain a minimally professional atmosphere without much to decorate or refine the place with. However, the dresses that sits on the headless, armless, papier-mâché and wooden mannequins are magnificent. Quality dresses, some made for women of a more modest income, while some made for women of a higher station. Although we see this distinction in the dresses, it is obvious that both kind have been made with craftsmanship, an eye for detail, and a lot of love.*

HANNAH. And I still can't convince you to come
  with me?
ESTHER. I admire the people of your faith, Hannah.
  But I don't feel it like you do.
HANNAH. I know. But America. It could be a new
  start for us.
ESTHER. Edenbridge is my 'ome. It's always been my
  'ome. It's been yours, too.
HANNAH. I—I never belonged here. Except with you.
ESTHER. Are you sure about this, Hannah? I know
  you believe in this, but—America is so far.
HANNAH. I want to be with my people.
ESTHER. I thought I was your people.
  (There is a knock. HANNAH *and* ESTHER *look at each*
  other, confused.)
HANNAH. Who could that be at this hour?
ESTHER. I'll get it.

(ESTHER goes to the door. In the door frame stands a regal woman in a hooded cloak.)

ESTHER. Can we — can we help you, Miss?

> *(The woman takes back her hood to reveal GEOR-GIANA. Her expression is hard, icy, a calm exterior just barely concealing the wild fury underneath, the heat in her eyes. Without so much as waiting for an invitation to come inside, she makes her way in, almost pushing ESTHER out of the way to do so. She carries a valise with her.)*

M'lady, this is a surprise. It's looking pretty murky outside. Would you like some tea to warm you up?

GEORGIANA. Do not put on your false kindnesses with me, you hypocrite.

ESTHER. This is about Stephen, isn't it?

GEORGIANA. You ought to call him Sir Lockhart.

> *(Intimidated into silence, ESTHER watches as GEORGIANA as she makes her way around the shop inspecting it with condescension and arrogance. GEORGIANA walks amongst the mannequins. She stops at one particularly beautiful dress and stares it down.)*

Headless. Armless. How appropriate.

ESTHER. Miss?

GEORGIANA. *(With a touch of tendernesss.)* I almost pity them.

> *(She starts gently touching the dress, her fingers smoothly gliding down its fabric, feeling its quality and care, and she almost understands it for a moment. She looks it over, and we see her rare*

vulnerability come through once again.)

They have fashioned us into a thing of beauty, it is true. But with no eyes to see with, no arms to act. Blind and crippled. Is this what these men have created us to be?

(ESTHER becomes more and more nervous at this bizarre behavior. We see HANNAH approach, unseen by GEORGIANA. She looks as startled as ESTHER. In the meantime, GEORGIANA is almost in her own world of thought, as if the dress makers didn't even exist. It's just her and the dress.)

Or is it we who wanted it, who willed it? We — I. I so much wanted to be admired — beautiful. Did I allow this?

ESTHER. M'lady, I have ended whatever chances I could have had at Mr. Lockhart's heart. You can still —

GEORGIANA. I do not want to hear it! I do not want to hear your pities or your sympathies or your condolences!

ESTHER. You don't understand —

(GEORGIANA reaches into her valise and pulls out the dress which the dressmakers had created for her. ESTHER gasps, not at the revelation of the dress, but at the other object GEORGIANA pulls out: her father's dagger.)

GEORGIANA. Yes, you know every stitch in this dress — this horrid shroud!

ESTHER. We have meant you no harm!

(Having knocked, but unheard, STEPHEN enters unnoticed.)

GEORGIANA. Your sister so earnestly said that I was beautiful—you said that this fitted me! Well, have this for your troubles and cares!

(With very purposeful and skilled strokes, GEORG-IANA stabs into the dress and starts shredding it with the dagger. The Dressmakers watch horri-fied at this display of rage and deliberate destruc-tion. In an almost graceful fit of fury, GEORGIANA destroys the dress.)

I do not want your beauty! I do not want your dependence! I will not debase myself with your embarrassing costume any longer!

(ESTHER goes down her knees, touching the remains of the dress with some remorse. She then looks up, angry.)

ESTHER. For all your eloquence and fury, *m'lady,* you've become nothing but a jilted spinster.

(Infuriated, GEORGIANA harshly slaps ESTHER. HAN-NAH lunges forward grabbing GEORGIANA by the shoulder. GEORGIANA, in surprise and fear, twirls, lifting the dagger which slices through HANNAH's dress and into her upper arm. HANNAH screams and clutches her arm, as GEORGIANA steps back in shock. ESTHER rushes to grab some disinfectant and clean bandages and immediately begins to attempt to stop the bleeding. STEPHEN lunges to the dressmaker's aid.)

STEPHEN. Georgiana!

GEORGIANA. Stephen?

STEPHEN. Georgiana, have you lost your mind?!

GEORGIANA. Stephen, please, it's not how it looks—

STEPHEN. Then why do you have a dagger in your
hand?! If you want to vent your jealousy, come
at me! If you want to strike some one, strike me!
(STEPHEN *approaches* GEORGIANA, *and in an instinct
that surprises even her, she lifts the dagger against*
STEPHEN. STEPHEN *stops, shocked* GEORGIANA *wide-
eyed and afraid looks at* STEPHEN *defensively, but
then back down at the dagger. In a moment of
comprehension, she lowers the dagger and stares
back up at* STEPHEN. *Georgiana then turns and flees
out the door.* STEPHEN *turns back and helps* ESTHER
with HANNAH's *wound, as* HANNAH *winces and cries
in pain. Blackout.*)

*Fallon Hanson as Hannah Whitefield, Tatum Langton as Esther
Whitefield, Angela Youmans as Mary, and Margie Johnson as
Georgiana Highett. Courtesy of UVU Department of Theatrical
Arts.*

Jamie Denison as Georgiana Highett. Photo by Greg Deakins.

SCENE SIX

The Highett Mansion, the drawing room. A terrible thunder storm is heard outside. CATHERINE *enters with* DARREL *trailing behind her.*

CATHERINE. Get away from me! I told you not to
come here again!

DARREL. Catherine, darling —

CATHERINE. I am no longer your darling!

DARREL. What has gotten into you?

CATHERINE. I know, Darrel! I know all of it!

DARREL. What do you know?

CATHERINE. I know that you are a scoundrel and
that I will no longer be a part of anything that
you have touched.

(Exit CATHERINE. *Enter* THOMAS.*)*

DARREL. Thomas, my friend —

THOMAS. I am not your friend.

DARREL. You are my partner. Now you understand
that lovers, they have their little spats every
once in a while. Women can be so emotional.
Go to her, calm her down and tell her that I
just want to talk things through. I love your
sister, she must know that.

THOMAS. Love? Love! You love no one.

DARREL. Thomas, why antagonize me? We are partners. We are in business together.

THOMAS. We are no longer in business together.

DARREL. *(Quietly threatening.)* Oh, yes we are.

Many business partners dislike one another,
but they each have something the other wants.
You have my future and I have your past. Thus,
go get your sister for me.

(THOMAS doesn't move. DARREL storms:)

Go get her!

THOMAS. My, things certainly are unraveling for you.

DARREL. What are waiting for, you preening pea-
cock?

THOMAS. Sticks and stones, old boy.

*(Enter GEORGIANA. She is disheveled, rain soaked
and fierce looking. The dagger, which she still has
been carrying, is placed aside as she takes off her wet
gloves, cloak, etc. Upon seeing DARREL, her fury
becomes even more pronounced.)*

GEORGIANA. You — get out! Get out! Get out!

DARREL. Thomas, please, go get Catherine. It is
important that we are all here to discuss what is
to be expected of all of us.

THOMAS. Only since you said please.

(THOMAS exits.)

GEORGIANA. You slithering creature, what are you
plotting?

DARREL. You always assume the worst.

GEORGIANA. Only when you are around. You have
the smell of filth wherever you go.

DARREL. That scent was already here, Georgie. I just
uncovered it.

GEORGIANA. You do not get to call me Georgie.

*(Enter THOMAS with CATHERINE, who is reluctant to
return.)*

DARREL. Good. The whole picturesque family! Now
     listen, all of you. I am sick of this little dance,
     so I am cutting off the music and will be
     straightforward with you. I am here to propose
     a marriage. A marriage of convenience.

GEORGIANA. Are you serious? Darrel, will your
     arrogance ever cease?

DARREL. All you have to do now is decide whether
     its Georgiana or Catherine who marries me. I
     do not care who anymore, as long as I am tied
     to this family.

     (*CATHERINE goes to* DARREL *and slaps him.*)

CATHERINE. You already have a wife, you have a
     child! I will never—

DARREL. You tart!

     (*DARREL slaps* CATHERINE, *but much more fiercely.*
     CATHERINE *crumbles to the floor.* THOMAS *grabs his
     father's dagger and raises it against* DARREL.)

THOMAS. Do not ever touch her again!

DARREL. (*Cautiously.*) Don't you see where you are?
     I have much to offer all of you.

GEORGIANA. You are not in a position to offer us
     anything.

DARREL. Georgiana, please, tell your brother to lower
     the dagger.

GEORGIANA. If he did not grab it, I would have.
     After how you just attacked us, I would not
     care if he killed you dead on the spot. I would
     call it self-defense.

DARREL. You are an intelligent woman, you must see
     your family for what it really is. Look at how

Thomas threatens me. And your sister, she
provoked me. You think that I am the villain?
Your family is the greatest enemy you have.

GEORGIANA. They are no such thing!

DARREL. You truly think so?

THOMAS. I would talk less, if I were you.

DARREL. Do you think that Catherine and I have had
a pure, platonic relationship? Her reputation
would be ruined, if the world discovered her
secret life with me.

GEORGIANA. Catherine?

CATHERINE. Georgie — no, no, no, no —

DARREL. And Thomas! Now this will be a shock to
you!

GEORGIANA. Thomas is as pure as snow!

THOMAS. Georgiana —

GEORGIANA. Thomas —

DARREL. Naive! You are so naive! The great intellect, Georgiana Highett! The sentinel of wisdom is ignorant of what goes on in her own
house! Your sweet brother, your dear brother,
why, he is a criminal. He is guilty of embezzle-
ment, bribes, graft. Your whole fortune is now
caught up in illegal affairs.

GEORGIANA. Thomas?

THOMAS. It is all true. I am so sorry — so desperately
sorry.

GEORGIANA. What have you done with Father's
fortune?

THOMAS. You do not understand, Georgiana. It was
Father who got me started into the whole

wretched business!

GEORGIANA. Pardon me?

DARREL. The embezzling has been going on for years,
hasn't it, Thomas? Long before he ever knew
about it. Your father built you up on that kind
of money.

GEORGIANA. No.

DARREL. He overspent your inherited fortune nearly
two decades ago, so he had to find another
way. His eccentric 'hobby' was no hobby at all.
It was desperation.

GEORGIANA. I do not know what game you are both
playing, but none of that is true.

THOMAS. Georgiana—when Father first told me
about it, I was shocked, just like you are. But
then he pulled me deeper and deeper into it as
he got more and more persuasive. He said that
he was trying to save our family. By the
strength of his arm, by the strength of his wit!
But my wits hadn't a chance. Since his death,
I have been trying to pay it off, to get it all
worked out honestly again. I have been making
deals, agreements. I have still had to—borrow
small amounts, but you must believe me that I
am trying to work it all out!

DARREL. I have enough evidence to throw your
brother into prison. So, if you care for your
reputation, if you care for your brother, if you
care for your family's name and fortune—

GEORGIANA. Out! I will have none of it. I will not
be blackmailed by you, nor will I let you black-

mail my family. If I have to, I will grind you down with my own hands!

(*DARREL charges towards* THOMAS, *and wrenches the dagger from him and points it at all of them threateningly.*)

DARREL. Now all of you listen. I am a reasonable man. I do not want any of this to get messy. But I know your secrets. Forget any advances I made towards Georgiana or Catherine or anybody. I would not give a single shilling for such sirens anymore. I want in the profits of your business, Thomas, or I'll reveal everything.

(*GEORGIANA begins to laugh.*)

DARREL. Why are you laughing, you ugly gorgon?

GEORGIANA. You toad. You utterly worthless creature.

DARREL. Shut your mouth or I will cut it off!

GEORGIANA. Could you be more predictable? Our classic villain!

DARREL. Don't you dare tempt me too far.

GEORGIANA. Oh, you are such a brave man.

(*GEORGIANA laughs again.*)

DARREL. I am deadly serious, Georgiana.

GEORGIANA. No, you are afraid. Afraid and desperate. Harold Lowe told me what you are.

DARREL. I will reveal everything!

GEORGIANA. Do it then. Reveal everything. But I will tell you this, whether you do or not, it matters not to us, for we shall see you fall with us, *Mr.* Fredericks.

DARREL. Fall? Why, don't you see, I am at my high
point.

GEORGIANA. Until tomorrow.

DARREL. What do you mean by that?

GEORGIANA. I received a letter yesterday. Why, yes,
from Mr. Harold Lowe.

DARREL. From — from Lowe?

GEORGIANA. Yes, he does strike a chord with you.
Did you think I did not see you storm out after
he arrived at the Ball?

DARREL. He means nothing to me.

GEORGIANA. I was curious. So I wrote him with a
few questions. He wrote back and told me that
he was well acquainted with your black deal-
ings.

DARREL. He's a liar.

GEORGIANA. He knows all about your deceptions,
your phony title, your failing financial situa-
tion, and your desperation to find capital to
save yourself with. He had a list of your trans-
actions and past history — why, I believe nearly
every one of the seven deadly sins were includ-
ed — and tomorrow in his paper — which, as you
know, is read by a multitude in London, he is
going to publish an article, an exposé of sorts.
He is going to publish it about you, Darrel.

DARREL. You are lying.

GEORGIANA. No, by the terror I see come upon you,
I see that you believe me quite readily. Oh,
our great oppressor! The great monster
Grendel! Where is your triumph now?

DARREL. I will kill you all!

> (*GEORGIANA goes directly to* DARREL *and places herself right at the dagger's point.*)

GEORGIANA. Then thrust the dagger, Darrel! But be ready for the curse that will come upon you afterwards.

DARREL. You do not frighten me with your curses.

GEORGIANA. You are nothing. A lie. Not even real.

> (*DARREL maintains his gaze with* GEARGIANA *as long as he can, until he trembles, and looks away for a moment. Then he looks up again with an empty, frightened gaze. He is near tears and we see something pitiable in* DARREL.)

DARREL. Georgiana —

GEORGIANA. Oh, such softness now? Are you really going to pretend you love me now? For I am about sick to death of man's fickle love!

> (*DARREL'S demeanor has completely changed. He does not seem threatening, nor even afraid any more, just an emptiness and loss that overcome him. Despite* GEORGIANA'S *statements otherwise, we see a bright glimpse of sad humanity within him, lost and wayward as it is.*)

DARREL. Georgiana — dear Georgie — aren't you as tired as I am?

> (*GEORGIANA is startled at* DARREL'S *meek pronouncement.* DARREL, *more out of exhaustion than fear, drops the dagger and exits. There is a long pause.*)

THOMAS. Bravo, Georgiana.

CATHERINE. Why, you were magnificent! We are saved.

GEORGIANA. No. We certainly are not "saved."

THOMAS. You bruised that serpent's head! You
smashed him! He will not dare threaten us
again!

GEORGIANA. No.

CATHERINE. You have sent him into the dark where
he belongs.

GEORGIANA. No, no, you don't understand. He was
not the real enemy, he was not—

THOMAS. There is nothing to—

GEORGIANA. There was no letter! There will be no
article!

CATHERINE. What?

GEORGIANA. I made it all up to frighten him away.

THOMAS. Why, it was a bold, convincing choice—

GEORGIANA. No.

THOMAS. You have given us our future back. You
have given us—

GEORGIANA. No! Stop it! I do not want any more
of your reassurances of smooth roads and
conquering opposition! Look at me, look at
yourselves. We have been revealed!

CATHERINE. No one need know—we can still get
through this.

GEORGIANA. None of us is wholesome or worthy!
Stephen was right to cut himself off from us!

THOMAS. Georgiana, calm down.

GEORGIANA. I have been calm my whole life,
Thomas! I have been been full of an arrogant
smugness as our lives have been threatened
and our principles have been prostituted.

THOMAS. We have won. You have won, Georgiana.

GEORGIANA. Won what? My dignity, my confidence? What have you won, Catherine, your virtue? What have you won, Thomas, your personal honor, your integrity? We are no better than Darrel Fredericks! We have our own sins to answer for!

(*CATHERINE goes and embraces* GEORGIANA. *GEORGIANA struggles, trying to tear away, which makes* CATHERINE *cling to her even tighter. They collapse,* GEORGIANA *sobs and shakes with intense emotion.*)

GEORGIANA. I have nothing left but this wretched face and proud heart!

(*They continue in this position as* THOMAS *sinks into a chair, now knowing full well what he has led his family into. His eyes are empty, nearly emotionless, as he listens to the cries of his sisters. Blackout.*)

Margie Johnson as Georgiana, Brandon West as Thomas, and Amber James as Catherine Highett. Photo Courtesy of the UVU Department of Theatrical Arts.

Jamie Denison as Georgiana Highett and Amos Omer as Darrel Fredericks. Photo by Greg Deakins.

Amos Omer as Darrel Fredericks and Jamie Denison as Georgiana Highett. Photo by Greg Deakins.

Kevin O'Keefe as Thomas Highett, Sarah Stewart as Georgiana Highett, and Cabrielle Anderson as Catherine Highett. Photo by Bryn Dalton Randall.

SCENE SEVEN

The mansion has been stripped down, the expensive finishings and ornamentations are gone. All that remains is the portrait of Alexander Highett. Enter MARY, trying to carry in a large trunk which is obviously too large for her, huffing and puffing as she goes.

MARY. Blimey!

>*(MARY throws down the trunk and sits down on it, exhausted. Enter STEPHEN.)*

STEPHEN. Mary?

MARY. Why, Mr. Lockhart! Who let you in?

STEPHEN. Well, I actually let myself in. Nobody answered and so I thought all the servants were—gone.

MARY. So they are, sir. I am the last relic to leave. I have gathered my things.

STEPHEN. *(Looking amazed at the luggage.)* So I can see. Mary, that luggage is nearly as big as you are!

MARY. Call me sentimental, sir. I'm a bit of a collector of past memorabilia.

STEPHEN. *(Looking about at the bare house.)* My, they have had to sell nearly everything...

MARY. All auctioned off, sir. The house has been sold, too.

STEPHEN. The house! My poor friends.

MARY. Poor indeed. They'll have barely enough to scrape by for a while, especially compared with what they're used to. Their father's fortune, their father's busines—all gone.

STEPHEN. They must be devastated.

MARY. No, sir. Not at all.

STEPHEN. What do you mean?

MARY. I've never seen them stronger, sir—happier.

STEPHEN. Happier?

MARY. Aye. They weep and mourn, of course, sir, but I've seen something grow in them. Some-times it's better to get something new than to fix something broken, if you understand me.

STEPHEN. Georgiana—is she here?

MARY. I don't manage things here like I use to. I am on my way out. Are you here to—?

STEPHEN. I do not know why I am here. I felt— compelled.

MARY. I see.

STEPHEN. Mary, you know the Highetts better than they know themselves—I need your counsel. What would you say—how do you suppose— ah, blast. I do not even know what I am trying to say.

MARY. Do you love Miss Georgiana?

STEPHEN. There. You have hit the question.

MARY. *(Pause.)* Well?

STEPHEN. I—I do not rightly know.

MARY. Her heart's not some baby rattle for you to play with, sir.

STEPHEN. Yes. I see that.

MARY. Very good then, sir.

STEPHEN. So what do you suggest I—?

MARY. I don't suggest anything. I think it's about
time you all started making your own decisions. I best be going. Miss Georgiana's
been mighty fine to me. She's found me a new
position and is even having me driven over
there in a fancy coach—imagine me in a fancy
coach!

STEPHEN. That is wonderful, Mary.

MARY. But I've got to get my things down there—the
coach won't wait forever—and this beast is
heavy!

STEPHEN. Yes, it looks quite heavy.

MARY. If only I could find someone to help me.

STEPHEN. Well, we could call one of the butlers—

MARY. There are no more servants, sir.

STEPHEN. Well, then we could call the gardeners,
perhaps.

MARY. No more servants.

STEPHEN. But then the—

MARY. There is no one, sir. And I'm not a servant
here anymore either!

(Pause. STEPHEN *merrily winks at* MARY.)

MARY. *(Throws her arms up in the air.)* Oooh! No kindness for an old woman!

STEPHEN. Right, that leaves just me then, doesn't it?

MARY. *(Feigning resistance.)* But, sir—

STEPHEN. No arguments. Let someone serve you for
once. You just wait here and rest a bit.

MARY. Why, thank you sir, I—

STEPHEN. I'll be back in a moment.

(Exit STEPHEN *with the luggage. MARY stands in*

silence for a moment, feeling suddenly small in the big, empty house. Feeling awkward, as if she suddenly wants to be occupied, she takes off her shawl and begins dusting the fireplace mantle with it. She stops, places her hands on the mantle, and looks up at the portrait, overwhelmed with tender emotions, she weeps. Enter GEAORGIANA *and* HAROLD, *mid-discussion.* GEORGIANA'S *harsh and severe appearance is gone. Her hair is down and she is attired in a simple, but graceful dress that has a lightness to it. This makes her even more lovely than her ball gown did. Mary stands aside, unseen at first.)*

HAROLD. Georgiana, I can help! Why won't you let me?

GEORGIANA. We have already survived the worst of it, Harold.

HAROLD. Survived? I do not think you have any idea what you are in for, my dear. They have taken everything away!

GEORGIANA. Thomas is free.

HAROLD. Yes, they must have realized it was Alexander who caused this mess. Thomas did not deserve the full measure of the law to be thrown—

HAROLD. Do not deceive yourself, Harold. It was only Thomas inheriting the barontcy that saved him. Justice was not what we received—and I am grateful for that. We both know that Thomas should be in prison. As it is, we are lucky to simply be stripped of our property to pay the debts.

HAROLD. Come, live with me and my family. You, Catherine, and Thomas. I can help shield you from the elements.

GEORGIANA. No.

HAROLD. Why are you being proud about this? This was not your fault!

GEORGIANA. None of us is an innocent in this matter, Harold. It is time for us to make our way in the world. We need the elements.

HAROLD. Georgiana, I hope you know that if I had any idea of what Alexander was doing, I would have done everything in my power to—

GEORGIANA. I know, Harold. He fooled us all.

HAROLD. Please, let me know if you re-consider. I want to help.

GEORGIANA. You already have—my friend.

(Exit HAROLD. GEORGIANA *finally sees* MARY.)

GEORGIANA. Mary?

MARY. Pardon me, Mum.

*(*MARY *becomes emotional again.* GEORGIANA *goes and embraces her.)*

GEORGIANA. Oh, Mary—I understand.

MARY. No, no, you don't! Miss Georgiana, you'll have to go through many more years and much more experience, many more years, before you understand a heart like mine! But I don't mean to chide—don't mind the tears of a sentimental, old hen, Mum.

GEORGIANA. Mary, I wish—

(Enter STEPHEN.*)*

STEPHEN. The coach is ready for you, Mary—ah.

(STEPHEN and GEORGIANA are both very surprised to see each other. A long, tense pause.)

STEPHEN. Georgiana.

MARY. My, my, I believe that's my cue!

(Embracing GEORGIANA one last time.)

I love you, deary. Goodbye.

(With an impish smile.)

Imagine — *me* in a fancy coach!

(Exit MARY.)

GEORGIANA. So.

STEPHEN. So.

GEORGIANA. *(Simultaneously.)* Stephen, I —

STEPHEN. *(Simultaneously.)* Georgiana, if only —

(They both stop.)

GEORGIANA. You must understand that —

STEPHEN. I hope that —

(They both stop. Then they smile sheepishly.)

STEPHEN. You — you look absolutely splendid, Georgie. You know, I do not think I've seen your hair down like that since we were children.

GEORGIANA. So you are not angry with me anymore?

STEPHEN. Would it matter, if I was?

GEORGIANA. I think it might.

STEPHEN. Then no, I am not angry. You were under a lot of strain. Are you angry with me?

GEORGIANA. No.

STEPHEN. Then where does that leave us? At the beginning?

GEORGIANA. No. We can never go back to the beginning.

STEPHEN. Why not? Georgiana, think back to when we were children. It was so much more simple then, was it not? The love we felt for each other back then was so simple.

GEORGIANA. Love?

STEPHEN. *(Taking her by the hands.)* Can we not go back to it?

GEORGIANA. *(Pausing, then taking her hands gently away.)* No. We must go beyond it. Stephen, what of the dressmakers?

STEPHEN. What of them?

GEORGIANA. Is—is Hannah all right?

STEPHEN. The wound looked worse than it was. After we stopped the bleeding, she was fine.

GEORGIANA. Good. Very good. Are you—have you promised yourself to—?

STEPHEN. No. I no longer have any romantic intentions towards—either of them. They have been true friends, nothing more.

GEORGIANA. *(Afraid, but hopeful.)* But—then are— are you still going to America?

STEPHEN. Yes. I leave to Liverpool tomorrow and then off on a ship.

GEORGIANA. To follow your God?

STEPHEN. Yes.

GEORGIANA. God is stripping me of all my comforts.

STEPHEN. Georgiana—if God is truly the God of those that mourn, of those acquainted with grief, if He is truly the God of the downtrodden and the outcast—then you are closer to Him than you have ever been in your life. You are now in His domain and His sphere.

GEORGIANA. Edenbridge did not have room for either of us, did it, Stephen?

STEPHEN. Perhaps we outgrew it.

GEORGIANA. Just as we outgrew each other.

STEPHEN. Georgie, do you really think—

GEORGIANA. No, listen to me for a minute. You say you loved our life when we were children. Well, life is more complicated than it was and we cannot change that. I sometimes think that somewhere along the line that you may have saved my soul, but—

STEPHEN. I think you saved mine—

GEORGIANA. I said *listen*. The day may come when we will see each other again in happier circumstances, but as for today, we are traveling to different countries and if we are to truly discover our purposes we must learn to let go of our—securities.

STEPHEN. Can we not travel to the same country? You with me, or me with you?

GEORGIANA. Not different countries, but different paths—

STEPHEN. We'll merge them into the same path.

GEORGIANA. Different *realms*, Stephen. Before you came to me with such commitment and determination—don't lose that. You saw clearly then, see clearly now.

STEPHEN. But, Georgie—

GEORGIANA. Let me go, Stephen. Follow your vision.

STEPHEN. I—of-of course. You are right.

GEORGIANA. Good. Good, you understand.

STEPHEN. Then—then this is genuinely goodbye?

GEORGIANA. For now.

STEPHEN. Do you think we will ever—

GEORGIANA. I do not know. Time will tell.

STEPHEN. Then this truly may be our last moment?

GEORGIANA. Perhaps.

STEPHEN. Then let me just say this—it was not a mistake.

GEORGIANA. The kiss?

STEPHEN. Not just the kiss—everything. Farewell, dear friend.

> (STEPHEN *takes her by both hands and presses each of them, one after another, against his lips.* GEORGIANA *fights against the emotion this token causes.* STEPHEN *stares into her eyes one last time and then exits. Pause. Georgiana gently smiles and looks towards the door.*)

GEORGIANA. You can come in now, Mary.

> (*No response.* GEORGIANA *goes to the door and looks behind it.*)

Mary?

> (MARY *is not there. This absence is poignant.*)

The world has changed.

> (*Looking towards the portrait.*)

One last thing—

> (GEORGIANA *goes to the portrait and scrutinizes it.*)

We were going to take you with us, Father—but now I suppose we must not.

> (GEORGIANA *takes the dagger from a bag she had*

put aside and places it upon the mantle beneath her father's portrait.)

You will remain here, in the house you fashioned for us. You are the cherubim to watch over this garden, and this will be your flaming sword.

(GEORGIANA turns to leave, but then turns and gazes at the house. She looks back at her father's portrait and the dagger. She lets out a short, gentle laugh, but then it catches in her throat, as she struggles with the threat that the laugh may become tears.)

No. No more crying. We are in another domain, another sphere.

(GEORGIANA exits. As the lights fade, a light on the portrait and the dagger remains until those, too, fade to black out.)

CURTAIN

Jamie Denison as Georgiana Highett. Photo by Greg Deakins.

OTHER PUBLISHED WORKS BY
MAHONRI STEWART
AVAILABLE FROM PROSPERO ARTS AND MEDIA

PLAYS
The Drownéd Book:
The History of William Shakespeare, Part Last

Legends of Sleepy Hollow

Manifest

Swallow the Sun:
The Early Life of C.S. Lewis

Jimmy Stewart Goes to Hollywood

The Fading Flower

Emperor Wolf

NOVELS
Farewell to Eden

A New Age of Miracles

POETRY
the wild path

Made in United States
Troutdale, OR
07/09/2023

11087240R10098